BYTE ME!

BYTE ME!

ROBERTA STEELE

Published by Telos Moonrise
(An imprint of Telos Publishing)
Prestatyn, Denbighshire.

Byte Me! © 2014 Roberta Steele

Cover Design: David J Howe
Cover Photograph: Robert Harkess

First Edition

ISBN: 978-1-84583-860-7

British Library Cataloguing in Publication Data. A catalogue record for this book is available from the British Library.

1

Sam slipped the last paperclip onto the end of the necklace, then threw the chain onto the desk. She drummed her nails on the battered wood in an arrhythmic clatter, then swivelled her chair to face the window. A row of identical Georgian roofs glistened greyly back at her through the misty rain, a street of student digs and office conversions for shady solicitors, accountants, and in the case of her own building, a theatrical agency she suspected of being a cover for high class prostitutes.

A car pulled up somewhere close outside. The engine and exhaust suggested something loud and expensive enough to be interesting, so Sam rose from the chair and peered through the window. A woman was climbing out the driver's side of an oversize Audi. She wore a suit that Sam guessed was worth more than her entire wardrobe, and heels that could skewer a small dog. The woman glanced at the front of several houses then walked towards hers. Sam's heart started to hammer in her chest. Was this the mysterious visitor she had been promised?

The previous day, Derek Hanshaw – who until a

year before had been Sam's boss and was still her mentor – had phoned her and offered her work.

'Doing what, Hanshaw?'

'What you do best, Sam.'

She could hear the grin in his voice. 'Spit it out, you old bugger.'

'You know I don't have any ladies working for me anymore, Sam. We need to dig up dirt on someone. There's a suggestion you might be able to play your particular angle on him.'

Sam sighed. 'Hanshaw, I did that once, on the –'

'Bollocks, and you know it.'

Sam snorted. 'Yeah, you got me. Please don't tell me he's sleazy, though?'

'Can't tell you anything yet. You need to be vetted.'

'What?'

'Apparently somebody wants to sniff your arse and make sure you're up to the job. Before you ask, I've no idea who. Two o'clock tomorrow okay for you? Your office?'

Sam had agreed.

Now she looked up to the fake station clock on the wall. Five minutes off the hour.

Even though Sam was on the second floor, the front door creaked loudly enough for her to hear it. A few minutes later heels rapped sharply along the uncarpeted corridor outside her office. A silhouette appeared on the frosted glass window of her door, and Sam was just drawing breath to call 'Come in' when the shape seemed to lift something to its face and fiddle with it for a moment. Only then was there a knock.

Sam settled for 'It's open' and tried to look like she was working on something. Heels clipped into the office, and the door shut.

'Samantha Taylor?' An expression of vague distaste settled into a woman's cultured voice. Not upper class, Sam decided, but trained.

'That's the name on the door,' Sam replied. 'How can I help …?' She had intended to add 'you' at the end of the sentence, but her lips stopped working. The woman was stunning. Not calendar-girl pretty. She was a decade older than Sam, maybe a little more, with chiselled cheekbones that came only from breeding, not a scalpel. Her hair was dark, wound tightly into place with clips and clasps, and her lips were painted with a red so rich it was more blood than cherry.

What made her stand out even more was the domino mask covering the upper half of her face. It was black, possibly leather from the way it moulded to her face as soft and supple as the finest calf skin. A dozen spots of light outlined each eye in an Egyptian curl, and at the outside corner of each a larger gem sparkled. Black feathers, frilled, swept back from the sides of the mask. The woman's eyes sparkled more coldly then the gems surrounding them, a deep violet that Sam guessed to be from contact lenses. Even so, the effect was startling, and evocative.

Sam swallowed hard and motioned to the chair opposite her. The woman looked at it and seemed to be considering dusting it before she sat. Once she was settled, she crossed her legs with a soft rustle that made Sam think of silk, and suspenders, and possibly a Basque. She noticed the woman was wearing gloves, and wondered how far up her arms they went.

'You are the private investigator?'

'I am.'

'I expected someone older.'

'I look younger than I am.' Sam realised the woman was putting her on edge and tried to relax. It wasn't easy. Something radiated from the woman, but Sam wasn't quite sure what. It was more than confidence, though.

'I don't expect you will have references to hand, but I will need to know more about your professional qualifications.'

Sam bit back a snappy response. The woman was patronising her and, worse, had taken over the meeting. Sam didn't like to be led, but the bitch obviously had money. If she wanted to engage in a little wealth transfer, Sam would have to play long.

'I've been a licensed investigator for three years, and had my own business for a year. I've been instrumental in three successful divorces and one criminal indictment for embezzlement...'

'Is that all?'

'I didn't think you would be interested in the minor cases.'

'I see.' The woman picked an invisible speck of lint from her skirt. 'You may be adequate for the task I have in mind.'

'Why don't you tell me about it so I can decide if the agency wishes to take it?' Sam's teeth locked together as she tried to shut herself up. Her heart was blup-blupping in her ears and she could feel dampness under her arms.

'In good time. First I need some kind of guarantee about your discretion.'

'We treat all our customers' information with the utmost –'

'Guaranteed by what?'

'I'm sorry?'

The woman took a deep breath. 'By what means can you guarantee that my business with you will remain confidential. Surely there is some professional body ...?'

Now, as well as controlling the meeting, the woman was talking down to her in the manner of a headmistress. Sam felt a curious tightening in her gut as the thought flickered across her mind, but she ignored it. This was going too far, and she was beginning to wonder if she really needed the money this badly.

'Lady, you get my word. In this business, anybody who doesn't play by the rules gets a bad reputation, and bad news travels fast. If I was in the habit of gossiping about clients, I wouldn't have any. Now, how can I help you?'

The woman locked eyes with her, and Sam had to fight the urge to apologise instead of returning the gaze. 'Very well. I assume you are aware that I have engaged the services of Hanshaw Investigations, who have recommended you?' Sam nodded. 'I require that between you, you supply me with sufficient evidence to enable me to remove a certain businessman from his position.'

'Go on,' Sam prompted when the woman didn't seem inclined to offer anything more.

'Is the instruction unclear?'

Sam took another deep breath, trying to make it discrete. Four bloody words, but delivered with such disdain that Sam's initial reaction was to reach across the table and slap the woman. The same tightness flickered across her belly, and as she drew in another breath she felt the fabric of her blouse scrape across her nipples. Barely noticeable through her bra, but enough to snap her back to the moment. The last thing she needed was to get distracted now. She mentally slapped herself, but it didn't really help.

'No, ma'am, it's not. But at the very least I need the name of the target. The more personal information you can give me, the less I have to find out for myself and the quicker I can be productive. Background information too.'

'How tedious, but if you insist …'

'I'm afraid I cannot take the case without it.'

'Very well. The man's name is Simon Cornell. The company is Cornell Software Solutions.'

'Company address?'

'Really, all this information has been provided to Mr Hanshaw.'

Sam hesitated for a heartbeat. 'Fine. Then what can you tell me about him?'

'We have no social contact. I find him quite tedious.'

'Really? Why is that?'

The woman launched into a comprehensive character assassination of the target, covering a range of misdemeanours from dangerous sports to womanising. Sam took notes on autopilot, most of her attention focusing on something far different. First, the woman's voice had a mesmeric quality. Secondly, Sam was trying to analyse and control her body's unexpected reaction to the snobbish woman's presence.

At first she had tried to deny it, but she was turned on. In fact she was positively horny. What troubled her was that she was not quite sure why. Sam had a healthy libido and would have been amongst the first to admit it. She knew men found her attractive, although she had never quite figured out why, and she wasn't afraid to use her body in the line of 'duty'. Admittedly, she usually tried to keep it down to winsome smiles and fluttering eyelashes, but there had been occasions when she had used an offer of sex – usually accepted – to get what she needed.

She even flirted, briefly, with other women. Sam had found sex with women to be an interesting diversion, but little more. It was something she didn't seek, but at the same time did not dismiss as a possibility if the right opportunity came along.

So the big question still remained; why and how was this awful woman giving her the hots? Her body language was neutral, and the only eye contact she had made had slivers of sharp ice running along it. Her attitude was domineering, and she was in need of some lessons in good manners. Sam still had no answers. She was jerked back to reality by the woman's slightly raised voice.

'I said, is that all?'

Sam scanned quickly through her notes. 'I think so,' she muttered, then noticed something. Apart from the minor detail that most of what the woman had told her was rubbish, she had glossed over the one comment that was of interest to Sam. 'You mentioned Mr Cornell has something of a reputation as a ladies' man?'

'The fool is a rake,' snorted the woman. 'Apparently he rarely spends a weekend alone, and always with a different woman.'

'I take it this is anecdotal? You have no first-hand knowledge of this?'

'Of course not. I told you, I can barely speak to the man. He makes no secret of it, however.'

'Is there any pattern to his behaviour?'

'He has a favourite club, I believe. The Globe or some such. In Walthamstow. He gets most of his girls there.'

Sam wondered how the woman knew this, but realised she wouldn't make any headway if she pushed back on the point. She decided it was time to close the meeting down. 'Thank you. One last question before we move onto my rates: why do you want to get rid of him?'

'I thought you were to pry into his business, not mine.'

'I have to know what sort of evidence I have to get. Setting him up for indecency is not going to help if he's embezzling you.'

There was a frosty pause. 'You have a point. Cornell set the company up eight years ago, partly with his own capital, partly with money advanced by a silent partner. When that partner died five years ago, I bought the shares from his widow on the understanding I would be an equal, active partner. Despite the man's every effort to stop me, I have doubled the size of the business since I took over. I have an opportunity to push the business further, but he's preventing me from doing so.'

'Isn't it a little extreme to hire me to get rid of him? I mean, this is a management dispute.'

'He refuses to see sense. I have even tried to buy him out.'

'And is there anything specific that triggered your visit to me?

Another hesitation. 'He plans to float the company on the stock exchange.'

'But you said you are equal partners.'

'Almost equal. He holds 51 percent of the existing stock. If he is determined to go through with the floatation, I cannot stop him, and my position could become weaker. Now, can I assume you will work on the case with Mr Hanshaw?'

'So long as we can agree terms.'

'My agent has already negotiated a deal with Mr Hanshaw. No doubt he will come to some arrangement with you. I trust that will be acceptable?'

'All right. How do I contact you?'

'Why would you wish to?'

'Progress reports? To report the successful conclusion of the investigation?'

'You will report to Mr Hanshaw. He will report to my agent.'

The woman rose to her feet, straightened her already immaculate skirt and walked to the door. As she put her hand on the doorknob, Sam threw out one more question.

'Can I ask why you came to me? I mean, why the face to face?' Sam decided not to mention the obvious lengths the woman was employing to disguise herself

'Whilst Cornell is a lecher, and will chase after anything young and female, I needed to ensure that you were pretty enough to be sure of catching his eye, and intelligent enough to do understand what is required. On both counts you appear… adequate. I also need to ensure that you will do anything – anything at all – to achieve the required result. Are we clear?'

'Absolutely,' Sam replied, coolly. The woman's attitude and assumptions nettled her, even though she was right.

'Then this is the last time we shall see each other. Any attempt at communication other than through my agent will be deemed breach of contract, and there will be penalties.'

The door closed and Sam slumped back in her chair with relief. The meeting had lasted only 20 minutes, and yet it had felt like an hour and had been an ordeal she did not care to repeat. She stretched languidly, then realised she needed to go to the bathroom. Locking the office door behind her, she scurried downstairs to the ladies' toilet.

A smudge of shiny dampness stained the gusset of her panties. Sam stared at it in disbelief. Surely the snooty bitch hadn't turned her on that much? She passed an experimental finger between her legs, and it slipped easily between the moist lips of her sex. It came away glistening with her fluids; she stared at it for a moment, unwilling to believe what she saw, then repeated the motion just to be sure. This time her finger brushed lightly across her clit and she had to bite back a moan as the brief contact sent an unexpected flash of pleasure through her. The finger seemed happy where it was and doing what it was doing so she let it carry on, opening her legs wider. Her other hand reached up to gently stroke a nipple, and an image formed in her mind. Breasts and masks, a hand in hair pulling, forcing a head downwards. The sordidness of where she was mixed with harsh voices, demanding voices. There were no bodies, no faces, just concepts, and she couldn't have said whether hers was the hand or hers was the hair. A gentle orgasm rippled through her and she tried not to make a sound. Thumping her forehead lightly with the palm of her hand Sam caught her breath then returned to her real reason for visiting the ladies room. She had surprised herself. She had done a sleazy thing or two in the past, but masturbating in the office toilet was a new one. She flushed the loo, washed her hands, and gave the air freshener a quick squirt before grinning at herself in the mirror and returning to her office.

2

The following morning Sam stopped by her own office just long enough to knock up a sign for the door, explaining her absence with a lie and to beg prospective customers to ring her on her mobile. Then it was time to pay Derek Hanshaw a visit.

She had spent the previous night trying to convince herself that the deal was not going to go through and that the woman would change her mind and go to someone else. Despite her attempt to be professionally pessimistic, she had slept poorly and had been as wound up as a child on Christmas Eve. Regular work, especially for a client like this, would sort out all her outstanding bills and feed her for the better part of a year.

Even while she had been telling herself not to get involved until she had seen Hanshaw, Sam had not been able to stop herself from doing some preliminary research. The internet was the best thing – or maybe the worst – that had ever happened to the investigation business. She had already been through Cornell's company website and seen his recent tax returns. An impressive number of hits got thrown up when his name was entered into her favourite search engine; sport, charity, community – a regular philanthropist. Also one of the oldest covers for someone up to no good.

When she arrived at Hanshaw's offices she wandered into reception and waved a 'Hi' to Joy, Hanshaw's receptionist. Joy was a stereotype. She loved the '50s look and always wore her hair up, a cravat, and wide, winged spectacles. There was a rumour that she and Hanshaw were an item, but nobody had been able to prove it, and nobody had ever got drunk enough to ask. Joy pursed her cherry red lipstick at her and shook her head. 'He's with someone.'

'Client?'

'Tony.'

'Buzz him anyway. Pleeeeeeez? It's to do with the new job.'

Joy looked suspiciously at her over the top of the pink frames, then shrugged. 'He can only fire me once.' She reached for the button on the old intercom and spoke so loudly into the microphone that Hanshaw must have been able to hear her even without it.

'Can't a man get any peace,' the tinny speaker complained. 'Send her in, then I can get rid of her quicker.'

Sam blew Joy a kiss and opened the door to Hanshaw's inner sanctum.

There was a reason her own office looked so much like Hanshaw's. As far as she was concerned, it was the way they were supposed to look. The room smelt of cigar smoke, even though Hanshaw wasn't supposed to have smoked in there for at least the last five years. The single light-fitting with a fly-shit-spattered shade in the centre of the ceiling was the only source of light in the room apart from a small lamp on Hanshaw's desk. The window was firmly closed, and looked as though it hadn't been cleaned since the first moon landing. Along one wall were three dented metal filing cabinets, and Hanshaw's desk dominated the space near the window. Basic and battered, it was the first thing you saw as you opened the door, and the only three chairs in the room clustered on either side of it.

'I heard that,' Sam said as she walking into the room. 'So what's the deal with this mystery bitch you sent to interview me?'

'Bitch? That mousy little nobody?'

'Five-ten without heels, dark hair, statuesque, expensive taste in suits and cars?'

Hanshaw rubbed his chin as Sam dropped herself into the chair next to Tony Ferrioni. 'Interesting. Obviously not the same woman.'

'Mine said her agent was negotiating with you,' said Sam.

Hanshaw snorted. 'Negotiating! Rich. She came in, told me what I had to do and how much I was going to get paid for it. Made to walk out when I tried to "negotiate."'

'What are you being paid?' asked Sam, and grinned when Hanshaw showed her two fingers. 'Well, I had to try. What am *I* getting paid?'

'Your usual day rate, of course, for any day you actually work on the case.'

Sam let silence negotiate for her.

'All right, double,' Hanshaw finally conceded.

'Come on, you penny-pinching git. I'm guessing you screwed her good on the rate. I know how you ramp things up if it seems like a punter can afford it.'

'Double plus expenses?'

'Triple, plus expenses.'

Hanshaw threw up his hands in mock despair. 'You trying to ruin me, woman? Double rate retainer until the case is resolved or you're fired. Reasonable expenses.'

'Done,' said Sam and leaned forward with her hand outstretched. 'Where do I sign?'

'You don't,' said Hanshaw, and the grin he had worn during the negotiations faded to a look of mild concern. 'This is a no records case. No names. Nothing.'

Sam cursed inwardly that she hadn't held out for more; no records meant cash, which meant a good chance of confounding the Revenue. It also meant Hanshaw would have stuck an even bigger premium on the rate he was bleeding the client for. Still, it was done now, and she was going to be making plenty – especially if the case dragged on.

'Where do you want me to start?' Sam asked.

'Your side of the investigation is your own. You've played this trick before. Oh, there's one thing. Background check on his uni. Warwick. You'd fit in best for that.'

'Okay. E-mail me the details. Anything else on this guy.'

'Just this.' Hanshaw opened a file on his desk and passed her a four by six inch photo. 'This is what the guy looks like, just so you don't get any moody images off the net.'

The picture was ideal for identifying someone, a crisp three-quarter profile. The man looked to be in a good mood, perhaps on the edge of smiling or laughing. Perfect teeth, lightly tanned, unremarkable hair in a short style. He had no body art and wasn't wearing jewellery, at least not that she could see.

'Can I keep this?'

Hanshaw waved at her, and she interpreted that as a yes. 'Just get out of here and let me work,' Hanshaw grumbled.

Sam ruffled Tony's hair on the way to the door – earning her an outraged 'Hey!' – waved goodbye to Joy, and set off to Walthamstow for a meeting she hadn't arranged yet.

All Sam wanted was actually to meet the man. Not, she knew, the correct sequence according to the *Everyday Little Manual of Snooping*, but the approach had worked for her before. The trick was finding the right situation, and she had already thought of that too.

Walthamstow was only a half hour drive from her office. She looked scathingly at her battered VW Polo, rust-blotched and wearing its years and miles heavily, and thought of yet another use to which she could put some of Hanshaw's money.

The Polo got her to the car park of the Globe Bar and Club at a little after 1.30 in the afternoon. She was not impressed. The place looked to have been built sometime in the '70s; squat and ugly, looking not unlike a warehouse, or maybe a failed retail unit. The car park was oversized – who would want to drive to a club? – and with only the front bar open, the place looked deserted.

She found the door to the lounge and walked in. Her shoes stuck slightly to the carpet as she stood at the bar, hinting at years of spilt pints and neglect. The few patrons huddled in one corner looked as though they had just walked off a building site. Sam, still in the business suit she usually wore to the office, felt very conspicuous and cursed herself for not checking the place out for more than its address.

A bar girl, about the same age as Sam but with higher mileage and make-up overdone to try to hide it, finally noticed her and ambled over. 'What can I get you?' she drawled in an apathetic Essex accent.

'The landlord or manager, please,' said Sam, pasting on her best friendly smile.

The barmaid's expression went from bored to suspicious. 'What you want him for? You got nothing to complain about. Nobody's done nuffink wrong.'

Sam briefly wondered if it was the environment or her incompetence that made the girl so defensive, but kept her happy smile pinned in place. 'I've no complaint. I'd just like to talk some business with him, if he can spare me a moment or two.'

The suspicion changed to a sneer, and Sam guessed she had been reclassified from 'possible threat' to 'sales tart'. The girl wandered slowly off down the bar. She ambled back a few minutes later, followed round the corner of the bar by an unwholesomely fat man who wheezed audibly as he walked.

'What do you want?' he growled before he even reached Sam, his voice rattling with a 60-a-day habit and the miasma of cigarette smoke wafting before him, unusual in the new era of health police.

'Perhaps we could go somewhere a little less public?' Sam suggested.

The manager grunted and pointed to a door at the end of the lounge. 'Through there.'

Sam opened the door and found the 'club'. Daytime made it look dingy, dirty and uninspiring. The windows were blacked out and the space was lit by strip lights in the ceiling. A bar ran along one side, stretching almost the length of the room, and at the far end was a platform for the band or DJ's decks. At the other was an inadequate seating area. Chairs clustered around tiny tables that looked as though they would wobble enthusiastically. There was also some seating arranged as wall alcoves. Sam bet there had been plenty of fights over who got those, and that they were where the majority of the dealing went on.

The fat man squeezed himself into one of the booths as she looked the place over. 'Again, what do you want?'

'Your help,' Sam replied, sliding into the seat opposite him and handing him one of her business cards.

The manager read it then threw it back on the table. 'I don't know anything.'

Sam left the card where it had landed. 'I didn't ask you a question. I need an excuse to be in this place on Friday and Saturday nights, for the next couple of weeks, on and off.'

'The door charge is 20 quid, or free if you dress sexy enough. Open to over-21's.' He started to lever himself out of the seat.

'I don't want to look like I'm on the game,' said Sam, letting her voice get a little harder, 'and I don't want to be stuck out here with the proles ...'

'The what?'

'Proles ... y'know ... Never mind. I'll give you £200 for every night you let me work behind the bar.'

The manager froze, then oozed back into the seat. 'Why?'

'Not your problem.'

'Ever worked behind a bar before?'

'Yes.'

'How long ago?'

'A few years,' Sam lied. She had helped out in the student union bar, and her maths had been such a liability they had eventually restricted her to collecting glasses.

'You'd be useless. Five hundred a night.'

'Two-fifty.'

'Four.'

'Three and stop wasting my fucking time,' snapped Sam. 'I've already seen four counts I could get Licensing to screw you on, and from the stench of fags coming off you, you're obviously smoking on site. You'll make up to two grand just for letting me stand behind the bar.'

The manager stared hard at her. There were beads of moisture on his face, but Sam knew they weren't because he was feeling any pressure. He would have a couple of boys, or girls, a whistle away who would happily put her in hospital for a week. The silence stretched uncomfortably and Sam was expecting him to tell her to bugger off.

'Minimum of a grand, three hundred a night. When do you want to start?'

'Tomorrow night?'

'White blouse, tighter the better, black everything else. Be here by seven. And try not to make it too obvious you're useless.'

'Do I look that stupid?'

The manager squeezed himself out from behind the table and walked towards the door. 'Ask me again tomorrow,' he said without looking back.

Sam wanted to wash her hands, but guessed that the toilets would leave her feeling worse than she already did. She left the club and headed for the motorway. Now that she had arranged the first part of her plan she had a little shopping to do. She had a very specific style she wanted to wear in the club, and she couldn't do it with her existing wardrobe.

3

Ryk had a problem with the little slut. He was trying to treat her like anybody else whenever he encountered her in the office, but he was finding it more and more difficult with each passing day. To know so much that was sordid about both her and her mistress, his boss, was a trial to him. Having to resist the temptation to tell somebody else, to spread it around the office to all the brain-dead no-hopers with their common little wives and girlfriends. 'Look,' he wanted to scream. 'See how she trusts me and not you? See how she rewards me and not you?'

He held his tongue.

Partly this was through fear. His boss had already shown him the material she would release to the police if he blabbed – material showing him to have psychological issues and implicating him in something that involved children. It was solid, air-tight, and utterly believable – and on a 'dead man's switch' to release automatically if anything happened to her.

It was all lies, of course. But *this* was real. It was happening right now. He was following the girl down a hallway in his boss's extravagant house. She was wearing a tight maid's outfit, impossibly high heels and seamed fishnet stockings. The shoes were locked onto her feet and she wore a leather-lined steel collar and cuffs, again all locked into place. He ached to know more about what she and his boss got up to, and was sure that what he got to see was only a tiny corner of the full picture.

That was how he had been 'recruited'. An anonymous e-mail pointing him to a link, which routed him somewhere else, until all the clues brought him to a video feed of the girl in front of him. Contact was established, promises were made, and his life changed.

They stopped at an ornate double door that looked like it came out of some old movie. The whole house screamed of crass wealth, and the smell of affluence made Ryk feel giddy as he dreamed about what he would do when he got his share. The slut-maid knocked on one of the doors then opened them in response to a muffled command from within. They walked into his boss's study. The slut walked up to the queen bitch, curtseyed deeply, and announced him.

'Mr Ryk Richards to see you, mistress.'

Ryk felt his dick stir and tried to think of his hated maths teacher naked.

'You may stand behind me,' the mistress said to the slutty maid.

'By your mercy, mistress,' the maid replied and took up position.

Ryk loved the way they talked. His boss was an ice queen, compressing an unbelievable amount of contempt into her voice whenever she addressed the girl. On the other side, the girl's submission was absolute.

'Good afternoon, Mr Richards. You may deliver your report.'

'Everything's just fine, miss. No problems at all.' He put on his best 'trust me' smile.

'I want a report, Richards, not a postcard.'

Ryk flinched. 'Sorry. The imaging software works perfectly. Still working on the delivery agent, but we are on track for it to be delivered on time.'

'How do you know the imaging solution is so perfect?'

'I tried it out.'

'Fool.' His boss's voice chilled still further and Ryk suddenly felt the urge to piss.

'I was careful.'

'On whom did you test it?'

'Claire, in the office. I wiped it off her system as soon as I was done though.'

'Rash and dangerous, Richards. You are to do no further testing on the system without consulting me first.'

'Of course, miss.'

'And what were the results?'

'Wonderful. I infected her computer with the meme virus and added a payload for someone eating chocolate. She went out at lunch and bought a huge bar, then stopped what she was doing to eat some each time the virus triggered.'

'That could be coincidence?'

Ryk shook his head. 'No chance. I triggered the image 15 times after she had bought the chocolate. She reacted every time.' He let out a snorting laugh. 'Bet she felt sick by the time I finished with her.'

'Please, Mr Richards. Spare me your adolescent humour.'

'Sorry.'

'Now, the other matter?'

'Almost there. There are still one or two packages that might pick it up, even though they couldn't stop it.'

'Unacceptable. The whole strategy is based on nobody ever knowing the agent exists.'

'I know. We can fix it. I just need time.'

'This project has already taken longer than I had hoped. I have interested parties lining up for a demonstration, and you are delaying me, Mr Richards.'

'Really? Who?' said Richards, then cursed himself for opening his mouth.

'That is none of your business. You are being amply rewarded, financially and otherwise. Focus on those areas that are your responsibility.'

'Yes, boss.'

'You sound less than grateful, Mr Richards. Are you unhappy with the financial arrangement? Or is it perhaps that you do not find my slut to your liking?'

'No, honestly. I'm really happy.' Ryk back-pedalled as hard as he could, terrified that he might upset the bitch enough that some or all of his rewards might be taken away.

'I am so glad to hear it. Curiosity can have such unfortunate side-effects. Wouldn't you agree?'

Ryk nodded enthusiastically. He had no intention of crossing her. She terrified him. His imagination had already supplied him with several additional and terrifying ways she could ruin him and he had no intention of giving her an excuse to come up with something worse. Of course, if he could find out where she had hidden her 'dead man's switch', then things would be different, and his imagination had furnished him with several scenarios to match that too.

The woman took a moment, then gave him an enquiring look. 'Nothing more?'

He shrugged. 'We're still secure, and nobody has any idea what I'm working on.'

'Good. I believe we need waste no more of each other's time. I assume you wish to take your bonus in the usual way?'

'Absolutely.'

The maid had known this was coming. It happened every week; the brief meeting, then the invitation she dreaded. Still, it was for her mistress and she was usually rewarded afterwards. Her mistress waved her forwards then twirled a finger. The maid put her hands in the small of her back and turned away. There was a metallic click and she knew a padlock had linked her cuffs. A tingle ran from the small of her back to her clitoris. Even a simple restraint like this was sufficient to arouse her. There was a tap on her arm and she turned back to face her mistress and her visitor. The pathetic little man already had a leash in his hands and clipped it to her collar.

'I believe you know the way,' her mistress said to Richards, dismissing them. The man pulled her from the room, almost dragging her across the hall to the small drawing room he was allowed to use. The maid, whose real name was Karen, stood with her face lowered, waiting for the diatribe. It was not long in coming. Richards grabbed the leash near the collar and lifted her head until she was looking into his face.

'Mine now. Might not be for long, but you're mine. Open your legs.'

Flecks of spittle peppered her face as he ranted at her. She parted her legs as instructed, trying to make sure the smug little grin hovering just behind her lips didn't become too obvious. What was coming was not going to be pleasant, but it was for her mistress, and to serve gave her a warm feeling deep in her soul. That it was something she disliked actually made it better, in a way, and there was always the hope of a reward later. He broke her little daydream of anticipation by shoving his hand into her crotch.

'Bitch has done it again,' he muttered, then raised his hand as if to slap her across the face. She looked straight into his eyes, knowing that the blow would never land, or that if it did Richards would pay unimaginably. She didn't understand why he was so upset. Every week he found the same thing. Her mistress was very careful with her property and had no intension of seeing it ruined by an amateur. That was why the maid was wearing a stiff leather bra and a studded chastity belt. Richards could neither molest her nor punish, and would just hurt himself if he tried. His punishment would be swift. Mistress had promised her that.

Richards pushed her to her knees. The next phase of the disgusting man's ritual had begun. He was so unimaginative that the girl found him almost comical. On the other hand there was a broad streak of cruelty in him that would have frightened her if she had not been under the protection of her mistress. He grabbed her hair and pulled it until she looked up at him again.

'Just wait. When I finish this job I'll get you. No strings, no leather bra, no protection. You'll be mine. Your precious mistress promised. Then you'll really find out what it means to be a slave.

She kept her face straight somehow, and even tried to put fear in her eyes. Another lie. Her mistress had told her about the arrangement she had made, but also that she had no intention of honouring it. The girl's heart skipped as beat as she suddenly hoped it was Richards who was being lied to and not her, then she felt guilty for not trusting her mistress.

The man lacked any finesse, and gave her no opportunity to use her skills at oral sex. She could have blown his mind, if he had let her, even though his prick was so short and scrawny he couldn't even make her gag with it. All she could think of was getting the horrible event over as quickly as possible. There were still a few tricks she could use, even on him, and within a minute or two it was over. Richards pulled his underpants and trousers up and stormed out of the room. She waited until she heard the front door slam, then rose to her feet and made her way back to her mistress's study. The doors were awkward with her hands still fastened behind her, but she had had a great deal of practice.

Mistress said nothing as she walked into the room, but immediately released her wrists and handed her a glass of orange juice. She gulped it down greedily. It didn't entirely take the taste of Richards' prick from her mouth, but it took the edge off it.

'Thank you, mistress.'

'No, thank you. I can imagine how distasteful servicing that man must be for you.' She handed the girl a key. 'You have an hour and a half to yourself. Take a nice bath then come to my rooms.'

'By your mercy, mistress,' she said, curtseying again. She walked sedately out of the room, glowing inside. Her mistress had spoken to her almost as an equal, something she only did when she was proud of her. As soon as the study doors closed she hurried as fast as the shoes would let her back to her room. The key released everything, and while the bath filled with bubbles and scented water she brushed her teeth and used a depilatory on her sex and underarms. The bath was pure heaven and she languished shamelessly in her reward.

To the minute, she knocked on the door of mistress's bedroom. As she had been given no other instructions, she was naked and unfettered. Permission was given to enter and she walked in. Mistress was nowhere to be seen, but steam drifted from the *en-suite*.

'Put on the blindfold, then stand by the bed.'

The blindfold was on a chair. The girl put it over her eyes once she was stood in the right place and waited, wondering what her treat would be. She heard mistress pottering around in the room, then felt hands pushing her down onto the bed. She sat on the edge then lay back when the hands pressed her again. The hands guided her once more and she lifted her feet from the floor, letting her thighs fall open and expose her as she drew her knees back. She felt deliciously exposed.

Fingers touched her sex, spreading a tingling lubricant across her labia and clitoris, even down to her anus, then again on her nipples. They tightened impossibly quickly, almost painfully, and the tingling of the cream on her sex made her ache to touch herself, made all the more wonderful by the knowledge she must not.

Footsteps again, getting closer, then something began to nudge between her legs. No, *two* somethings. Karen moaned happily as she guessed what was to come. The first dildo engaged itself in the folds of her sex, penetrating her slightly. A brief pause, then the second dildo pressed up against her anus. With gentle but relentless pressure the two shafts buried themselves into her. She cried out as her back arched and she fought not to come. She was stretched open, impaled by mistress. More pressure as mistress settled onto her then leaned forward. First a kiss to the nipple, then words whispered in the ear.

'Come as you please.'

Fingers closed around nipples and pulled harshly. She screamed and surrendered to her first orgasm.

As soon as her shaking stopped, the dildos began to vibrate and pulse, and mistress began to fuck her with long, slow strokes. Gradually, the tempo and ferocity increased until the two women were pounding against each other. Karen wailed loudly as the second orgasm swept over her, much stronger than the first, leaving her limp and lifeless on the bed.

Mistress slowly withdrew the two phalluses, and Karen dimly listened as she bustled around the room for a few moments. Then she felt the mattress move beneath her. Cool hands took her wrists and placed then over her head, then the mattress bucked again as a thigh settled on each side of her face, pinning her arms to the bed. She jumped, the noise of the sharp slap startling her more than the sting as a crop tapped her leg. She spread herself, quickly, grateful the warning had been so gentle. The soft scent of Freesia and pussy got stronger, and she eagerly opened her mouth as her mistress settled onto her face. She could still breathe through her nose, but her mouth was sealed. She let out a squeal as the crop landed again, closer to her crotch this time, knowing it aroused her mistress. As fingers tightened on her nipples, she reached up with her tongue and parted the lips of her mistress's sex.

Her mistress came twice before she climbed off the maid's face, and the girl offered no resistance as she was slid across the bed and helped under the covers. The blindfold was removed. Tonight she would sleep the arms of her beloved mistress, an honour to be relished. Tomorrow, reality would return.

4

Sam showered and dressed earlier than she needed to, then ended up fussing endlessly with the outfit and almost making herself late. It was intended to get her noticed, but not to make her look too much like she was trying to pull. The skirt was pleated, not straight, and a little shorter than it should be. Well, the manager had said black. He hadn't said anything else. The white blouse was workaday, but a little tight. With the seamless bra, that would leave punters wondering if she was wearing anything underneath. Her tights were black, as stipulated, but opaque and with just a hint of shine. It was the shoes, though, that had given her the biggest problem. All the other girls would be wearing ballet flats. Part of her wanted heels, but she would be on her feet all night and heels would make her stand out as unusually tall. She didn't want to be that obvious. She settled on a pair of patent Mary-Janes.

When she checked in the mirror she saw a pretty girl with a slight make-up and dress sense problem, who almost certainly didn't realise that what she was wearing was slightly more provocative than she thought. Perfect bait for a rake.

The landlord leered openly at her when she arrived, then waved her to the hatch at the end of the bar. 'I could get you a better job in a different club, if you need some cash,' he suggested, then laughed as she flipped him the finger. 'At least you had the sense to get here early. Debbie can show you where everything is and how the tills work.'

Debbie gave her a surly look. 'You didn't say you was looking for a new girl. I've got a friend who –'

'Shut your mouth. Who runs this place? If I want to hire someone, you think I'll fucking check with you first?'

Debbie's face paled even in the dingy light behind the bar. 'Sorry, Mr Wade. I …'

Sam took a mental note to watch her back. This wouldn't be a relaxing place to work.

The greasy blob was still venting at Debbie. 'If she can't pull her weight by the end of the shift, I'll dock it from your fucking pay.'

Sam thought about stepping in, but decided it was going to be for at most a half dozen nights. The last thing she wanted was for Wade to go back on his deal and ask for more or, worse, bar her from the place completely.

Debbie gave Sam a quick tour of the bar. She reeked of hostility, but the tour was comprehensive and accurate, as was the explanation of the till. 'It's idiot-proof,' Debbie explained. 'So long as you can remember what the twat at the bar ordered, it adds it all up and even tells you how much change to hand back. Keep the order in short chunks; don't let them reel it off all in one go.'

The tour over, Sam put herself at the end of the bar farthest from the doors and waited. Debbie did something under the counter and Michael Jackson's

'Beat It' thundered deafeningly around the room for a moment until she adjusted the volume to a more bearable level.

The first two hours dragged, but it was a Friday night and from ten the club slowly came alive. Now that the strip lighting had been replaced by a haphazard collection of spots and rotating light effects, the place transformed into a halfway decent club.

Sam was bored beyond reason, and had actually been back twice around the tour Debbie had given her, trying to remember where things were for later. The DJ had arrived at nine, taken an hour to set up, and was now doing his sound check over the top of the mix Debbie was playing. The cacophony of mismatched sound threatened to give Sam a headache, until she realised that Debbie had disappeared to the pub. Sam joined her and was reluctantly introduced to the other bar staff. None were any friendlier than Debbie, and Sam forgot their names almost as soon as Debbie said them.

The trickle of punters became a flood of girls in short skirts and hooker heels, giggling across the room at testosterone-fuelled boys posing against the bar. Sam had to start working, and found it difficult to keep up with the orders as she scanned the crowd for her target.

And then he was standing right in front of her, next to be served, asking for a diet coke with no lemon and putting cash down on the bar. He stood out like a wolf in a flock of sheep, radiating maturity and energy, stylish and confident. He was being looked at from every corner of the room; hungry looks from the girls who fancied their luck at bleeding a sugar-daddy, angry looks from the boys who realised a class above them. They resented him for being unfair competition.

'You new?' he asked when she brought back his

drink and change.

'Started tonight,' she replied.

'Good luck. Things can get a bit manic in here after midnight.'

'Thanks for the warning,' said Sam, and flashed him a broad smile.

She left him to his drink, watching him covertly as she served other punters. She was not doing too badly considering, and had so far messed up only one order. Debbie and most of the staff from the pub were working the other end of the bar; being closer to the door the pressure was heavier there, but the press was moving gradually towards her like a slow-motion wave.

Cornell was splitting his time between sizing up the incoming talent and ogling her. Every time she looked up, there was a 50-50 chance she would see his head in the process of turning away from her. As soon as she could spare a few minutes, she wandered back up to him and offered to refill his glass.

'Are you a regular?' she asked when he declined.

'Pretty much. I drop in most weekends.'

'Do they get much trouble here?'

He shrugged. 'Not that I know of, but I tend not to stay that late.'

Sam pulled a face. 'Great. Haven't worked behind a bar for ages and now I get thrown in the deep end.'

'Baptism by fire,' Cornell agreed and saluted her with his glass.

Sam was called back to the busy end and, after a while, lost track of Cornell. She caught one more sighting of him that evening, dancing with a girl probably not yet out of her teens. Sam stuck with it until one in the morning, then had to concede that Cornell had almost certainly left. That was her cue to do the same, and she arrived home some time after two.

It had been the most exhausting evening's work she could remember; her feet were killing her, her legs ached and her eyes felt as though something was behind them, trying to force them out of their sockets. She let her clothes fall where she dropped them and collapsed onto her bed within a minute of locking the front door.

When she woke the next morning, the first thing that crossed Sam's mind was that she would have to go back to the club that night. She groaned and pulled the quilt over her head, enthusiasm for starting the day draining by the second. A moment later she realised that there had been bright light streaming in through her bedroom window, and she cautiously allowed an eye to scout briefly out from under the bedclothes to check the time. It was already gone 11. Sam reluctantly pushed the quilt off. Muttering curses, she threw the previous night's clothes into the washing machine then, after only a brief pause to organise a mug of coffee, threw herself into the bath.

She scrubbed. Hard. The stench of stale beer and secondary perspiration filled her nose and made her gag. She had to wash her hair three times before she could believe it was clean. Once she felt a little more human she put on a robe and organised some brunch. Now she could spend some time thinking about how things had gone at the club.

The evening hadn't given her much to go on, and she realised she might have a problem. Her first impression of Cornell was that he was a nice guy. He was reasonably good-looking and had a fit body. He dressed well, spoke well and danced well. During their brief conversation he had been friendly. Not at all the wolf-lecher Sam had been expecting.

Beating up nice guys did not really sit that comfortably with Sam. To a degree, it went with the job, but it was something she preferred not to do. Unfortunately, Mr Cornell was not the one putting cash in her hand on a regular basis.

A slice of toast froze mid-way between plate and mouth. This was going to take too long. She wanted to get to know him, get inside his head. Playing barkeep for him would take weeks to get to that level of intimacy. But what if she pushed it? She knew he was interested in her from the way he had been scoping her in the club. Why shouldn't she bring it all forward, take the chance?

Sam wallowed around the flat for the rest of the day, ironed her 'uniform' and reported for duty at the club. Gus Wade drew her aside almost as soon as she walked through the door.

'How much longer are you wanting to do this?'

'Bored with my money already?'

'Your money I like just fine, but the other bar staff are edgy. The word is you're good with the punters, but it's obvious you've never worked bar before in your life. One of them already asked me if you were an undercover cop. I don't want rumours like that getting around.'

I bet you don't, Sam thought. At the first serious whiff there was a cop in the joint all the dealers would shut up shop and Wade's payoff would dry up, as would any kickback from the pimps who undoubtedly had girls working the place.

Sam nodded. 'Fair enough. I don't want to cause

you any more trouble than I have to. We'll call it an even six hundred and I'll be out of your hair tonight.' She thought for a second. 'Tell you what. We can help each other out. When I've done what I have to do, I'll break a glass. You throw me out, loudly. Make a big scene of firing me. That'll back up what I'm doing, and it should sort things with your staff.'

Wade considered the idea. 'All right, but it has to happen tonight. No later than 11. I don't want my staff on edge and I don't want them starting any more rumours there might be cops in the club. Now get behind the bar and stay out of trouble.'

Sam put on a miserable face as though she had been given a bollocking and sulked at the far end of the bar until the clientele started to arrive. The other staff bunched into a knot at the far end of the bar and, from the occasional glower flicked in her direction, it wasn't difficult to see she was the main subject of discussion.

Cornell walked in at exactly the same time he had the night before, heading first towards the centre of the bar but very obviously changing direction when he saw her. She shone a bright smile at him. 'Good evening. Coke?'

'You've a good memory.' Cornell returned an easy smile. 'Something for yourself?'

'I think I'll join you with one of those. Still a long night to come. Last night nearly killed me.'

'I thought you were doing rather well,' said Cornell and sipped his cola.

Sam was impressed. If it was an act, he had put just the right amount of nonchalance into the comment. 'Thanks,' she said, and flashed him another smile. 'I got clumsy, though. Dropped three glasses in an hour.'

'You'll get your hand back in.'

'If I stay here that long.' Sam grimaced. 'At the moment it's a toss-up to see if I quit before I'm fired.'

Cornell chuckled and was about to speak when Sam was called away to serve another punter. Trade began to pick up, more quickly than on the Friday, and Sam found she had little time for anything more than snatches of conversation with Cornell. She did notice one thing, though; Cornell was staying put at the bar, and seemed less interested in checking out the incoming female flesh.

Sam checked her watch and saw that it was a little past nine. It was early, but that might work to her advantage; if Cornell hadn't picked out a target, she might stand a better chance. Trying to make it look like a fumble, Sam dropped an empty wine bottle on the floor. It shattered with a gratifyingly loud crash and, from the corner of her eye, she saw Cornell wince sympathetically as half the club jeered.

Wade lurched out of his office as though he had been waiting for the cue and, after a few choice insults, loudly and publicly sacked Sam. Sam responded with a physically impossible suggestion and walked out, but not before she caught Cornell's eye and threw him a wan smile and a shrug.

She left the pub by a side door and stomped across the car park in a feigned fury, kicking at the tyre of her Polo before fumbling in her bag for her keys.

A voice called to her across the car park. 'Excuse me.'

Score! Sam made sure the angry expression was still on her face before she turned. 'What?' she snapped as she spun around. 'Oh, sorry. I thought you were someone from the club.'

'That's okay,' said Cornell. 'I'd probably be pissed

off if that had happened to me. I hoped I'd be in time to speak to you. Do you want me to have a word with the landlord? I've got a little influence with him. Might be enough to get you another chance?'

Sam pretended to consider the idea, then grimaced. 'Thanks, but I don't think I could go back in there if he came out on his knees and begged me.' Somehow Cornell seemed taller without the bar between them. She was 5′ 6, and the top of her head was lower than his chin.

'Good for you. In that case, can I talk you into letting me buy you dinner?'

'Excuse me?' Sam's tone edged towards frosty as she method-acted suspicion. Inside, she was struggling to keep it that way. Triumph was trying very hard to make her grin foolishly at the success of her idiotic plan.

Cornell raised placatory hands. 'I know I'm being a bit forward, but once I got here I realised I wasn't really in the mood for the club tonight. It's still early, we're both at loose ends, and I thought maybe you could use some cheering up. There's a great Italian five minutes up the road. We eat, I walk you back to your car, and you drive home. No strings.'

Sam had to admit he had a good line in chat, but at the same time got the feeling this wasn't his usual approach. He sounded a little unsure of himself, and some of the brash confidence he had displayed inside the club was missing. Then again, perhaps that also was his MO; to leave each conquest thinking that he was treating her differently, even though he was a human wolf. The point was, in any case, academic as he was doing exactly what she wanted him to. With only a slight show of reluctance, she agreed to join him.

The restaurant was very expensive and very crowded. 'We don't stand a chance of getting a table here,' Sam muttered. 'Besides, don't you think I'm a bit underdressed? I don't want someone thinking I'm staff.'

'We could try the drive-through burger joint down the road, if you prefer.' Cornell's face was deadpan when she glanced up at him. 'Trust me, you look fine, and I guarantee we'll get a table.'

They stepped inside and waited to be noticed. A comfortably padded man in a slightly stained apron bustled up to them, hands held out in welcome and a beaming smile on his face, babbling in a slightly overdone Italian accent. 'Signore Cornell. Welcome. You have a reservation? I don't remember seeing your name on the list for this evening …'

Cornell shook hands with the waiter, owner, whatever and Sam saw something slip from one hand to the other. 'Sorry, Louie, but I didn't book. My friend and I were passing and decided we needed to eat. I hoped you might be able to squeeze me in?'

Louie pulled a long face that was almost comical. 'Signore, on a Saturday night you ask me the impossible. Still, I will see what I can do.' He bustled away, leaving them conspicuously by the door.

Sam felt exposed, and fidgeted.

Cornell leaned forward and muttered, 'Don't panic. Louie has never let me down yet.'

A shiver ran down Sam's spine and she struggled not to let it ripple out through her body. His lips had brushed, butterfly soft, against her ear, and the touch had been electric.

Louie threaded his way back through the tables, his face wreathed in smiles that were almost religious in their intensity. 'Signore, signorina, you will come with me please?'

He led them between the tables and through the doors to the kitchen, babbling over his shoulder as he led them past bubbling pots and stainless steel benches. 'Such a thing! Never have I known it.'

He took them into a side room. It was bare apart from a scrubbed pine table, a few chairs and two pictures on opposite walls: one of Christ and the other of the Virgin Mary. Red gingham curtains had been drawn to drive the night from the window. An elderly lady, silver hair pulled back in the tightest of buns, dressed all in black and with eyes as sharp and bright as a fox's, stood next to one of the chairs. Cornell surprised Sam by bowing slightly to the woman.

'Mama, you are well?'

The old woman beamed a smile and nodded, then spoke in rapid Italian to Louie.

'Mama says she is most well and hopes you are too,' Louie translated. 'She says you çan eat here.' His voice became almost reverent. 'This is Mama's room.'

Cornell took Mama's hand and kissed the back. 'Tell Mama she is too kind.'

Louie again translated, and Mama smiled at Sam and patted Cornell on the arm before walking from the room. Louie and another waiter bustled about setting places at the table while Cornell held a chair out for Sam.

'What did he mean when he said this was Mama's room?' Sam asked, worried that she had kicked the poor old lady out into some uncomfortable storeroom.

'That lady is the family matriarch. She has the final say on everything that happens in the kitchen, and when she's not working, she sits in here. It's a great honour for us to be allowed to eat here, though the kitchen staff may not thank us. She will be in there, watching them like a hawk.'

The dinner was relaxed and the conversation light. Sam let Cornell do most of the talking. She found out that he loved rugby and Japanese movies but distrusted politicians and policemen. They shared some music tastes, but Sam spoke very little about herself as she was wary of giving anything away, and lies had to be remembered accurately. By the time they were lingering over coffee, she had come to the conclusion that she liked Cornell. If she was honest with herself, she didn't just like him, she fancied him. This was not going to make things any easier. As they left the restaurant and walked back to the car park, she made one last attempt to needle him.

'They warned me about you.'

'Who?'

'The others at the club.'

'Really? I'm famous! What did they say?'

'That you picked up a different girl every night.'

He shrugged. 'Not every night, but near enough.'

'Is that all this was? A bribe?'

'Is that what you think?'

Sam hesitated before she answered, and even stopped walking for a moment. 'No. Not exactly.'

'Good. It wasn't a bribe. I just wanted some company. And to get to know you a little.'

They had reached Sam's car now. Cornell was standing a little too close to her; not threatening, but intimate. She imagined she could feel the heat from his body in the chill night, and couldn't find an answering warmth within herself. She was feeling cheap, but couldn't put her finger on exactly why. True, he was nicer than she had expected, but this was a job, feelings shouldn't be coming into it. *Get a grip, girl,* she told herself.

'Are you doing anything next weekend?' he asked.

'Nothing planned.' It was an effort to keep her voice light yet interested.

'Then how about dinner at my place on Friday?'

Sam looked up into his face. A mistake. Her eyes locked onto his and she was unable to look away.

'P … perhaps.'

'I'll be here at seven. Meet me? In the car park?'

His face was very close now. She could feel his breath on her lips. Just another inch. She was never sure if she or he made the last movement. All she knew was that his lips touched hers and that he was soft and gentle; no brutal tongue, just a hint of openness, of more if she wanted it. And then he moved away and the cold filled the space where he had been.

'Next time,' he said as he left, 'the strings are optional.'

5

On Monday morning Sam got to work. Hanshaw had asked her to cover some of the routine grunt work on days she wasn't doing her own investigation, and that was fair enough – considering how much she was squeezing him for. She ducked the more mundane stuff, like credit checks. She wanted more information on the man, and to speak to people who knew him.

The Institute of Directors was not particularly helpful, but she did manage to get a list of professional bodies he belonged to. Padding naked around her flat as she made the calls, she managed to use the lie she was a journalist and that she was doing a profile of him to get a few phone interviews. Nobody told her anything she didn't already know or hadn't guessed, and she settled for setting up her visit to the university.

On Wednesday she took the train up to Warwick to meet with the man who had been Cornell's principal tutor. She missed the Polo, but it would have been unlikely to make both legs of the trip without assistance. She dressed conservatively for the occasion and decided to rely on fluttering her eyelashes to secure maximum co-operation.

Professor Godstone wore torn jeans, a T-shirt with artwork of zombies playing on the name Grateful Dead, and had his grey – but full – hair pulled back in a ponytail. His office was covered in books, mostly open, and Sam wondered if the man had ever heard of digital media. Sam fed him her cover story and he swallowed it whole. She then had to sit through nearly two hours of boring reminiscences and off-colour anecdotes, most of which were about the professor himself rather than about Cornell. When she could take no more, Sam pleaded another appointment and took her leave.

As she walked down the corridor, she heard someone call 'Hello?' It wasn't until the call was repeated and Sam heard footsteps approaching quickly from behind that she realised she was the target. She turned to face a woman about ten years older than her, rapidly slowing to a halt. Her hair was a wiry, unkempt mess, and her lack of make-up aged her. She was dressed in Oxfam-chic, but without much chic. Sam already had a thumping headache and really didn't want another chat.

'Can I help you?'

'I heard you're collecting information on Simon Cornell. Are you just looking for the generic crap, or are you actually looking to find out *about* him?'

They tucked themselves away in a corner of a refectory. The woman, now introduced as Candida Trent, sipped at a herbal tea. Sam had an extra-shot mochachino with marshmallows and two paracetamol.

'So how do you know Simon?' Sam asked, digging a notepad out of her bag.

'I was in his year. Most of his classes too.'

'What sort of person was he?'

'Up his own ass most of the time. But then, we all were.'

'What was it made you call out to me?' asked Sam. The verbal fencing could have gone on all afternoon as she tried to get to whatever it was Trent wanted to tell her, and she wasn't in the mood. If the woman didn't like direct, she didn't have to stay at the table.

'Not entirely sure. Partly because I know how Godstone likes to waffle on about himself. Partly because I'm the only other person here who knew him.'

'How well?'

'I was his girlfriend.'

Sam's ears twitched and she did her best not to lean forward too eagerly. 'What sort of boyfriend was he?'

'Difficult to say. I say we were together, but it wasn't really for long, and then he didn't get involved with anybody else in the uni. If there was a formal function, he and I would usually make an appearance together, but most of the time he was with off-campus girls. Never did get to the bottom of why.'

Sam let the conversation wander until the drinks were finished, then brought things to a close. She was in the process of shaking Trent's hand when something occurred to her. 'Do you keep in touch with Simon these days?'

'Haven't spoken to him for five years.'

'If the urge should come on you, please don't. At least, please don't mention me. The article is supposed to be something of a surprise.' And it could be rather difficult trying to explain to Simon why she was chatting up his old uni friends.

Trent twisted her fingers in front of her lips and winked. 'Not a word from me.'

Sam smiled and left, making a mental note to send a similar e-mail to the professor.

Cornell had not, it seemed, changed much with age. Even at university he had worked hard, played hard, and acquired a reputation for success with the girls. Not a breath of scandal or foul play, apart from the curiosity of him not mixing much with campus women. Trent had given her the names of a few that had been close to him, but she was beginning to wonder if it was worth following them up. Either Cornell was Teflon-coated or he really was the last of the knights in shining armour.

Sam got back to her office and found nothing helpful in the e-mail Hanshaw had sent her. It was written all in capitals and looked more like a telegram. Nothing on it made her life any easier. Everything was coming back as clean, clean, clean. Cornell's credit rating was impeccable, his business reputation was of being a stickler for contracts and fair play. He even bought the *Big Issue* from two different vendors, and his business funded a community outreach programme. Either she was missing something or they were chasing the wrong guy.

Thursday brought the final piece of info she had asked for, and it had been her last hope. Cornell had no criminal record, apart from an occasional traffic violation. Still, Sam decided there was a bright side to everything, including this. With all her other lines of investigation going pear-shaped on her, the only real source of information was going to be the man himself.

Now she had a good excuse to keep their tentative Friday appointment.

Sam decided to leave the car at home and took a cab to Walthamstow. After all, she could afford a little luxury now. Even though she arrived early, Cornell was already waiting in the car park. He greeted her warmly, but made no move to kiss her.

'Shall we go?' he asked almost immediately, and opened the door for her. 'Dinner won't be complicated, but I will need time to cook it for you unless you are tempted by a midnight snack?'

Sam laughed. 'Perhaps not. I'm already starving.'

She wasn't surprised to find his car was both flash and fast; she recognised it as a Jaguar, but that was as far as her car-knowledge went. Cornell drove quickly, but not aggressively, and Sam felt comfortable. So often it seemed a powerful car drove the man, not the man the car. This was different.

Cornell never spoke another word until they were on the M11, heading north. Then he said: 'May I ask you a personal question, Sam?'

'You can ask – I may choose not to answer.'

He grunted and fell silent for long enough that Sam wondered if he was having second thoughts. 'Fair comment. So, how do you like your sex?'

Sam snapped her head right to stare at him, almost giving herself whiplash, and felt her mouth gape open. All she could manage was a gurgle as her thoughts ran in circles. His directness and audacity astonished her, but intermingled with this she had to admit to a significant dose of admiration. She settled for a strangled 'What?'

'I asked you about your preferences when having sex.'

'I heard what you said, I was just having a problem ...'

Cornell shrugged. 'It's direct, I know. I've been told I should be more circumspect, but I don't like wasting time. Are you going to answer the question?'

'When you tell me why you want to know.'

'Do we really have to be so coy?' Cornell sounded surprised. 'I didn't expect you to ... Obviously because I expect we shall fuck tonight.'

Sam gasped again. 'Aren't we jumping to conclusions?'

'Are we? I thought it was obvious when I invited you last week. If not, please tell me now as we are about to come up to a junction, and it would a convenient place to turn around and take you home.'

'No,' said Sam, drawing the word out, trying to give the impression she was thinking things over. 'I don't think we need to go that far.'

'Good, now are you going to answer my question?'

Again Sam hesitated, fixing her eyes firmly on the floor and trying to get a blush into her cheeks. She could feel impatience radiate from Cornell and wondered if this was his Achilles Heel.

'I've never really thought about it in those terms before. I suppose I've always just sort of "done it". You still haven't told me why you asked.'

'Because I want to know if there is anything you particularly like or dislike; things that turn you on, or that you prefer to avoid. Better I ask than hope to stumble across them by accident, yes?'

'Good point.' She gave him a sly sideways look.

'Come on then, what turns *you* on?'

'Attitude, mainly.'

'What, like swagger?'

'Meaning I get turned on by an open mind and a willingness to expand on experience.'

'That sounds like you're softening me up for something weird,' said Sam, deliberately hardening her voice and leaning away from him.

Cornell laughed. 'Kink is in the eye of the beholder, Sam. It's all a matter of experience and preference. There is absolutely nothing on this planet that somebody somewhere won't find arousing, no matter what the rest of us think.' His face faded back to serious. 'Example. I get a kick out of seeing a woman dressed erotically; the kick is not in the clothes themselves, but in knowing that this particular woman thinks that what she is wearing is outrageously daring, that she is pushing herself beyond her normal boundaries.' He shook his head and laughed. 'Another failing of mine is a tendency to preach. Forgive me.'

Sam didn't get a chance to answer as Cornell was in the process of squeezing the car through a slightly narrow gate in a tall hedge. 'My home,' he announced.

At first Sam could see only a small bungalow cottage, cosy and not at all what she had expected. A moment later she realised that she had seen exactly what she had been supposed to see. Tall shrubs had been cunningly placed to hide the true extent of the building. Cornell stopped the car and opened her door for her.

'What do you think?'

'Clever,' Sam replied.

'You noticed, then?'

'Only just, but yes.'

Cornell smiled approvingly and Sam had the feeling that not many others had seen through the deceptive foliage. They went into the house and Cornell showed Sam to the lounge. She looked around and saw pretty much what she had expected to; clean and uncluttered décor with plain walls and paintings. Comfortable, functional furniture and state of the art technology.

She followed him into the kitchen, allowed him to provide her with a glass of red wine, and watched as a large ginger cat stomped out of the room, highly offended.

'Don't worry about him,' said Cornell. 'We have an arrangement. I feed him and he does what he likes. Always disappears when I bring company home.'

'Shame,' said Sam. 'I love cats but can't have one.'

Cornell started to fetch ingredients from various places around the kitchen, piling them onto the centre island. Sam watched him dice an onion with a very large, sharp-looking knife and decided he was skilled enough to talk while he worked and not lose any fingers.

'Do you pull that trick in the car with every girl you pull from the club?'

'Absolutely,' he replied, and Sam was forced to give him a point for honesty.

'Doesn't it scare most off?'

'Some. About one in four.' He paused for a moment and stared thoughtfully at the tomato he was in the process of quartering. 'Two reasons for doing it. First, it saves time. Gets rid of all the manoeuvring and posturing later. More time to focus on enjoying things.'

'And the second?'

'Shock factor.' He grinned, and for the first time

Sam thought she could see a predatory edge to his humour. 'Makes a girl think about her own sexuality. Seems to add spice.'

'Jeez, you make it sound so researched and methodical. Where's the fun of learning about someone, getting to know each other?'

'I did research it,' Cornell surprised her again. 'The idea came to me while I was at university. My degree was in computing, but I had a side interest in psychology.'

'Any plenty of willing subjects.'

Cornell laughed. 'Anything but. There was too much sex going around anyway, and the only girls I could have tried the idea out on were too intelligent and experimental already.'

Sam realised that Cornell had just explained Candida's story, and she tried to decide if she had just been insulted. She came to the conclusion that she had, but only in the role she was playing, so that was all right. 'Seems like all talk to me.'

Cornell chuckled. 'You should check out the wardrobe in the spare room.'

'Sorry?'

'I keep a few things around.'

Sam felt her lip curl. 'Second hand sexy –'

Cornell interrupted her, and there was an edge in his voice as though she had offended him. 'All new.' Again, he stopped what he was doing and looked at nothing for a moment. 'Mostly. Dry cleaned if not. Nothing sleazy.'

There was a tense silence. Sam let it stew for a minute then broke it. She had no intention of busting the evening now. 'Sorry. You really have thought of everything.'

'I like to try,' said Cornell, and took a sip from his wine. The tension lingered for a moment then disappeared.

Sam waited for Cornell to make the next move, but he seemed focused on preparing dinner. If she tried to move things forward, would she look too pushy? She was supposed to be working herself into his confidence, so what better way than to impress him?

'Would you like me to dress for dinner?'

To Sam's delight, Cornell fumbled the garlic press he had just picked up. It was only a small slip, but it was enough to let her know she had hit the mark. He stopped what he was doing and turned to face her. 'I would like that very much.'

Sam got the feeling that this was more important to him than she had thought. 'Is there anything in particular you'd like?'

'Yes, but I'm not going to tell you what.'

That was interesting. 'Why not?'

'I normally have another little lecture I give at this point, but I have this huge curiosity to see what you'll come up with on your own. I'll explain when we eat.'

'So where is this bedroom?'

'Through the lounge, down the hall, second door on the right. Dinner will be in about 20 minutes, and it won't wait.' He grinned hugely. 'And neither can I.'

6

Sam climbed down from the kitchen stool and wandered through the house. The spare bedroom was bigger than her lounge, painted in soft pastels and with an *en-suite*. The bed was king size, and the furniture was all white and vaguely Italian. There were two built-in wardrobes, both on the same wall and both with mirrored doors. One was locked but the other slid easily open and she began to investigate.

Sam found the collection rather tame. She was not exactly sure what she had been expecting, but what she found was available in most shopping malls – albeit from the shops mothers usually rushed their sons past. There were a few costumes – nurse, saucy student and, of all things, meter maid – but the vast majority seemed to be see-throughs and Basques. She *was* impressed by the collection of shoes arranged on a rack on the floor.

After all Cornell's bullshit Sam felt let down. Perhaps he really was nothing more than a lecher after teenage tarts. Still, she had offered to dress and she still needed to get inside this man's mind. She was also running out of time. She rifled through the wardrobe again and found a see-thru black dress that might have possibilities. She hurriedly stripped off her own clothes and slipped the dress on. The bodice clung to her torso, softly outlining her breasts without flattening them. The sleeves sheathed her arms, and the slit at the front went up to her navel so that the skirts parted on either side. There was nothing she could do about the dark triangle of her pubes, but her legs were too pale. She rummaged around through the wardrobe and found a pair of seamed black hold-ups. When she checked herself in the mirror, she grinned wickedly back at herself. Cornell was in for an eye-opener.

Sam made her way back to the kitchen, where Cornell had laid the table for two and the starter was already served. A sudden wave of shyness crashed over her. She was about to present herself to a man she barely knew, wearing something that made her look more than naked. She fought the urge to cover her breasts and sex, and forced herself to stand straight as she waited for him to notice her.

When Cornell glanced up he froze and took a long, hard look. Sam squirmed under his scrutiny, but felt her nipples tingle.

'Oh, well done,' he said, face coming alight. 'The dress suits you well. Erotic elegance. A lovely surprise, as is the absence of shoes. I probably ought to warn you I'm a Pisces.'

'So?' Sam did not pay much attention to astrology.

'We have a thing about feet.'

Sam giggled, but was astonished to feel her cheeks burning. Cornell pulled her chair out for her and she settled at the table. They feasted on pasta with an arrabiata sauce and ended the meal with real espresso coffees and an orange sorbet. The meal was perfect; delicious and enough to make her feel satisfied without being bloated. Sam was impressed.

The conversation had been neutral and surreal, and yet all the while Sam had been aware of Cornell's eyes on her breasts, and the way her nipples had responded to his attention. 'Do you always spend half the evening talking over your psychological theories with your conquests?' She knew it was a diversion.

'Never. And it's guests, not conquests.'

'Then why me?'

'You asked. Nobody ever asked before. Since you had the curiosity to ask, I assumed you had the wit to understand the answer.'

'I think that was a compliment.'

'It was. So is this. Has anybody told you how beautiful your nipples are?'

Sam choked slightly on the last sip of her coffee. Cornell chuckled and rose from the table. 'Here, give me a hand clearing up.'

It took only a few minutes to clear the table. 'What did you think of my little collection?' Cornell asked as she brought over the last of the cutlery. Sam did not answer, struggling with the alternative risks of offending him by telling him the truth, or equally by lying. Cornell looked up from the dishwasher, expression slightly concerned. 'Not to your liking?'

'Perhaps closer to say I was a little disappointed.'

'Why?'

'Well, after everything you'd said, I'd expected something a bit more ...' Sam tried to look as though she was looking for the right word. 'Extreme?'

'And you don't find sitting down to dinner with a virtual stranger wearing that dress extreme?' Cornell had an amused smile.

'Not really,' said Sam, surprising herself. 'Sexy,

yes. Embarrassing, definitely. But I was expecting to be shocked.'

'You have a wonderful knack of surprising me, Samantha.' He chuckled and muttered to himself. 'Disappointed.'

'So what are you hiding in the other wardrobe?'

Cornell's grin faded. 'Nothing important.' His tone suggested that was where the conversation needed to end, but Sam felt the need to push the point.

'So let me have a look. I may not be so disappointed.'

'Perhaps another time.'

Sam let it rest there. She had made her point, and there was an implied return visit. The last thing she wanted to do was spoil the evening. He had gone back to the dining table and was seated on his chair, pushed back from the table. Sam leaned against the island, the skirts of the dress falling open. 'So, what now, Mr Cornell?'

He held out his hand. Sam took it and he guided her until she stood in front of him. 'That depends on you. What would you like?'

'Something different,' said Sam, softly. 'Something new.'

'Turn me on.'

'What?' Not what Sam had expected to hear.

'Turn me on by pleasuring yourself. Touch yourself where you like to be touched, and how.'

Sam hesitated for a moment, then took her hand from his and took a step back until her buttocks were pressed against the dining table. Uncertainly, her hands moved upwards. Feeling dreadfully self-conscious, she cupped her breasts in her palms and started to run her thumbs over her nipples as she gently squeezed with her fingers. The soft material of the dress added an extra layer of sensuality to the pleasure and Sam's shoulders drew together.

Cornell's eyes were flicking between her fingers and her face, and knowing he was watching her every move sent tingles through her sex. Her hands released her breasts and each fingertip flicked across nipples grown achingly tight. Sam closed her eyes and let her head loll back as a soft groan drifted from her throat.

'Open your eyes,' said Cornell. His voice was quiet but commanding and Sam's eyes flew open. 'Don't stop,' he added in a softer tone, 'but you must keep your eyes open. Keep looking at me. Let me help.'

His hands went to her waist and lifted her so she could sit on the table. He moved his chair closer, so that his knees were just between her legs. Reaching forward, Cornell took each of her ankles, and lifted her feet onto his thighs, Sam's legs spread wide, leaving her deliciously exposed. Her finger found the lips of her sex again while her other hand teased a nipple.

'Have you ever made yourself come in front of a man?' Cornell asked, his voice low, hypnotic. Sam swung her head slowly from side to side and, for the first time, felt shocked. She was no stranger to sex, but masturbating was something she rarely indulged in – and then only in private. Unbidden, the memory of fingering herself in the toilet rose in her mind; the delicious debauchery of it, the sordidness. A shudder ran through her.

Sam slid her feet up Cornell's thighs, placing one either side of the bulge in his crotch and easing her thighs even wider so her sex would gape at him. As she slowly slipped a finger between her labia she let out another moan and her head fell to the side again.

'Look at me, Samantha. I want to see your orgasm in your eyes.'

Her middle finger began to press a little harder as she teased her clit. Her orgasm was quick and unexpected, ripping through her between one breath and the next. She had no idea if she had kept her eyes open, but she felt dizzy and started falling forward. Strong hands grabbed her shoulders and held her upright.

'That was beautiful,' Cornell murmured. 'Let me taste you.'

Sam looked up at him, confused.

'Your finger,' he said. 'Show me.'

She lifted her right hand, middle finger still shining with her juices, embarrassment crashing over her as he took her wrist and guided the finger to his mouth. He consumed it whole, sucking it clean, running his tongue around it, before allowing her to withdraw. 'Delicious.'

He took her hands and folded them across the small of her back, then eased her down onto the table until she was lying on them. 'Don't move your arms,' he whispered, shifting the chair again. She felt his hands around her ankles, lifting them, spreading her again, then his lips were around her clitoris, sucking hard.

In her post-orgasmic haze, the sudden touch was almost painful and she cried out as her back arched. She almost brought her arms out, only remembering not to at the last moment. As his lips released her she fell back to the table. She felt restrained, out of control. A moment later his tongue was fluttering delicately around the outer fringes of her sex, occasionally dancing along her inner labia, teasing them apart without probing within, slowly building up to a sudden deep plunge from just above her anus, through her labia, and across her clitoris.

She cried out, and again her body spasmed, but orgasm was denied her as he set about slowly teasing her again. She felt a finger dip between her labia, then it was pressed up against her anus. She braced herself for the penetration, but there was none – just a gentle pressure and sense of movement that soon left her wishing he would press just that little bit harder. Twice more he plunged his tongue deep into her sex, only to dance around the edges again, taunting her, teasing her. On the third time he flickered and flailed at her clitoris, driving her further and further until with a wail she came again.

There was a moment of discomfort, her legs dangling awkwardly over the side of the table. She tried to stir, her trapped arms making things difficult, and there was the sound of rustling fabric. A moment later hands were around her ankles again, raising them higher than before, then Simon was standing between her legs. 'I need a minute,' she tried to moan, but Cornell was already rubbing his cock against her sex to lubricate it. His hands shifted to the backs of her knees and he pushed into her with a slow, relentless motion. She moaned. He stretched her, but not uncomfortably so, and she felt very full. His balls came to rest on the cheeks of her ass and as he eased out of her she raised her ankles still further and arched her feet. She had no idea why, but it felt sexy.

Cornel set up a gentle rhythm, slow and steady, long deep strokes that seemed to reach into the very core of her body. The restriction of her arms made everything feel different, and as he drove her inexorably towards a third orgasm, she began to imagine phantom fingers tugging at her nipples, tweaking and pulling.

Cornell leaned forward, his rhythm became more insistent, then faltered. Sam realised he was starting to come, and her own orgasm exploded, filling her head with light and sound.

7

Simon Cornell looked down at the girl in front of him and shook his head. Just what the hell was it he had stumbled onto? He withdrew his rapidly-softening cock then gently rearranged his arms until he could lift her. She snuggled her head into his neck and murmured something he couldn't make out, but which sounded happy and sleepy. He had been going to carry her to the couch, but he changed direction. Holding her like she was made of glass, Cornell carried Sam through to the spare room and placed her gently on the bed. Trying to cover her with the quilt was too complicated, so he settled for draping his robe over her.

Making his way to the bathroom on slightly unsteady legs, he peeled off the condom, pissed, then smartened himself up. He put on another robe before returning to the lounge, in desperate search of coffee.

The coffee maker was still up to pressure so he filled the filter and clipped it underneath before pushing the button that started the magic. He slipped a cup in place just in time to catch the first drops, then took the espresso into the lounge. He felt he needed something bitter and intense to help his brain function. This woman was doing something to his head and he wasn't quite sure what. A frown started to pull at his forehead. What *was* she doing here?

She wasn't the type. He knew women, or thought he did; at least to the extent of being able to ensure himself a fuck or two every weekend. He would have bet good money that a woman like Sam would not have been such an easy acquisition. The girls he picked up from the club responded to being swept off their feet by his cash and his blunt confidence. Sam was smarter. It shouldn't have worked on her.

A little more analysis gave him the answer, at least a partial one. His usual routine had *not* worked. Mainly because he hadn't used it. It came as something of a revelation to Cornell that he had simply been himself. He could not remember the last time that had happened. He also could not remember the last time he had been tempted to open the second wardrobe on a first date. He chuckled to himself as he recalled some of the reactions he had seen when displaying his more exotic collection, but the smile was again replaced with a frown as he wondered what Sam's reaction would be. Assuming, of course, that he ever got the opportunity to find out. The possibility that Sam might not want to come back left a sour taste in his mouth that the coffee could not disguise.

He sipped the coffee, then grimaced and let it flow back into the cup. It was cold, and when he looked up at the clock he realised to his surprise that he had been mumbling to himself for almost an hour. He was equally surprised that Sam had not reappeared. He gave her another half hour, in which time he consumed another coffee and had a rare cigarette, shivering on the kitchen doorstep, before going to check on her.

The light from the hallway cast shadows around

the bedroom when he opened the door, and what he saw almost made him chuckle. The robe was piled in a heap on the floor but the outfit was nowhere to be seen. The girl was snugly tucked up in the bed, half the quilt under her, the other half folded over like a calzone, sleeping like a baby. After a moment, he decided that she might have the right idea. The washing up could wait until the morning. His robe fell to the floor and he slipped into the bed beside her.

The quilt being as it was, he realised the flaw in his plan instantly, and was just about to give it up as a bad idea when Sam stirred. Without her really waking, he managed to sort out the quilt, and as soon as he lay down, Sam rolled over and draped an arm across his chest. A stocking-clad leg slid up over his thighs. He found the sensation sensual, and was smiling as he closed his eyes.

The first thing that occurred to Simon Cornell was that he should wake up this way more often. Soft lips were kissing his left nipple and a gentle hand was working on his already erect penis.

'Nice,' he murmured.

'I thought you were never going to wake up. Want me to stop?'

'Hell, no.'

'Good, 'cos that's exactly what I'm going to do.'

The word 'What?' blurted from his mouth at the same instant as Sam's hand let go of his prick.

'To get you back for last night.'

'To get me back ...? Bitch!' He started laughing, even though there was a darker core to him that was resentful, angry.

'Is that any way to talk to a lady? Besides, I've got something better in mind.'

She produced condom in her hand like a magician revealing a coin, and moments later she was straddling him, stretching to reach beneath her to guide him. As soon as his cock was engaged, she sank down on him, quickly, making them both groan. As Cornell reached up to touch her breasts, Sam set up an insistent, driving rhythm. Cornell let her nipples run across the backs of his splayed fingers as she fucked herself on him.

Cornell exploded almost without warning. Perhaps it was the fact she was still wearing the clothes from the night before, or the way she was holding her bottom lip between her teeth, but his orgasm came upon him so unexpectedly he had no chance to try to delay it. Sam didn't notice at first, and he had to put his hands on her waist to make her stop before she broke something.

'Already,' she pouted, like some pony princess denied a party. He twisted sideways, throwing her onto the bed, then wrested with her until he had her hands above her head, held there by one of his. She had a 'What next?' look on her face, almost a dare. Fine, it was time to move her along a little, anyway.

'Open your legs.' He wasn't using his pillow talk voice. He was using his 'Do it now' voice. Not louder, just more intense. He saw a moment of shock in her eyes, then she pressed her thighs together. He ran his thumb across her right nipple, and watched her shoulders tense, then moved his hand to the left nipple and squeezed. 'Put your feet sole-to-sole and open your legs, or I'll pinch.' He added just a little pressure.

She blinked and her eyes opened wide. He wasn't sure if it was surprise at the position he was demanding of her, or the tone. He didn't really care. Her feet pressed against each other and her thighs fell open and she offered herself to him. Still pinning her arms above her head, he let go of her nipple and slowly traced his finger down until it was between her legs. He didn't penetrate her, just eased his fingers along her labia, teasing her clit. Her hips started to flex in seconds, and a moment later he felt her arms testing the strength of his hand. A smile twisted one side of his mouth. Even if she didn't realise it, she was entering the role, using the restriction to fuel her arousal.

He took the wet finger from her sex and touched it to her lips. 'Taste yourself,' he said, softly but insistently, pressing gently. He expected her to lick the finger, if she did anything, but her lips parted and she lifted her head to take the finger into her mouth. She pursed her lips around it and sucked softly as her head fell back. Again, Cornell wondered what the hell he had stumbled upon, and had to force his mind back to the moment.

With more insistent movements from his finger, he pushed her hard to an orgasm, keeping his finger on her clitoris and her arms pinned as she thrashed. When she slumped back to the bed, he kissed her, lingeringly, but without force. He could taste her sex, and felt his prick stir again.

'Nobody leaves my bed unsatisfied,' he said, smiling, but locking his eyes onto hers. She smiled back, but there was just a touch of uncertainty in her eyes. Good. He had pushed her.

'I need to pee,' Sam muttered. 'Do something useful. Make breakfast.'

Cornell found his robe on the floor and slipped it on as he walked to the kitchen. He had his back to the table when he heard her sit a few minutes later, and almost dropped the teapot when he turned and saw that she was wearing his shirt from the night before and a pair of white ankle socks. With her dishevelled hair and no make-up, it made her look charmingly girlish.

'Hope you don't mind me raiding the cupboard for the socks.'

'Of course not,' he replied. 'But why?'

'The floor in here is freezing,' she replied, but the look she gave him was curiously direct. He glanced down at the tiled floor, decided not to comment, and asked her for her breakfast order.

'Much to do this weekend?' he asked, cautiously. He was not normally a morning person, and didn't want to push any unknown buttons.

Sam pulled an unhappy face. 'Too bloody much.'

Cornell felt a curious sinking sensation in his gut and was surprised when he realised he was disappointed. Normally he simply called a reliable taxi firm and air-kissed his toy of the night at the door. He tried something he couldn't remember doing before. 'Shame, I was hoping you could stay longer.'

'I'd love to, but I really am up to my eyes in it.'

'You'd really like to stay?'

'Of course,' Sam replied, cocking her head to one side as if asking him why she wouldn't.

He must have let more of his surprise show on his face than he had intended to. 'So you had a good time.' God, why was he sounding so needy?

'Wonderful,' Sam said, grinning mischievously. 'I don't need to ask if you did. Incidentally, where did you learn to do that with your tongue?'

Cornell didn't understand her for a moment, then he felt his face start to colour as he hunted for something to say. 'Years of practice and iron willpower.'

'Willpower?'

'How else do you think I kept from sneezing as your pubes tickled my nose?'

Sam burst into laughter. 'Score one for you. Well, you can practise on me any time.'

'How about now?'

Sam's face screwed up. 'I desperately need a shower, and I really do have too much to do. Next time?'

'Feel free to make use of the *en-suite* in the second bedroom, and then I shall run you home.'

'Good. I won't need to give you directions for next weekend.'

'Eh?'

'Or were you planning on going to the club.'

Cornell rubbed his hand across his face. 'Why do I feel as though I'm not entirely in control of this conversation?'

'Because you're only a man, and men can't think straight for hours after they've had a fuck.' Sam smiled sweetly, waved, and ran off to the spare room.

The kitchen suddenly felt echoingly empty. He wasn't used to this sort of enthusiasm in the morning. A grin – which he guessed would probably look very silly from the outside – crept uncontrollably across his face as he came to the conclusion he could get to like it.

Later that afternoon Sam toyed with a glass of wine as she curled comfortably in her armchair. The weather was suitably drab for April, and cold enough that she felt justified in putting the gas fire on. Her laptop played random 'chilling' music from an online radio station, and she was thinking about the last 24 hours. Things had not gone as she had expected. She couldn't make up her mind if they had gone better, or too far.

Cornell had, as promised, driven her home. On the way he had found out that she was free on Wednesday, and had instantly pounced on the free time. He would pick her up at 7.30 and take her out for a drink. They kissed before she got out of the car – not passionate, but not a quick peck either, and she was left in no doubt that Cornell considered her more than just a casual fuck.

Sam wasn't sure how she felt about that. At a personal level, he excited her. She hadn't met anybody like him before; so confident, so in control of himself and what was going on around him. Time spent with him seemed different, and the sex …

From a professional standpoint she was breaking half the rule-book and ignoring most of the rest. She had a habit, a bad one she thought, of coming to a conclusion about a target's guilt very quickly. She was rarely wrong. In this case she would have staked what professional reputation she had on the hunch that Simon Cornell was one of the good guys. They weren't going to find any dirt on him because there wasn't any.

But now she still had to prove it, or prove herself wrong, and proving something wasn't there was always harder than showing that it was. Hanshaw wanted the money from this job. Fair enough; so did she. If he thought there was still information to be found, he would nag her to keep digging. If there was a bonus that involved finding something the client could use … Sam hated herself for thinking it, but she wasn't sure that Hanshaw wouldn't invent something.

There was more. She had gone in too deep, too fast. She had made an impression on the target, rather than staying out on his periphery. Observe from a distance, that was how she had been taught. Don't engage until you know what you're engaging with, or you could be grabbing a tiger by the tail.

Anyway, that was exactly what she had wanted to do. It annoyed her that since the moment she had offered to 'dress' for dinner, she had gone out of her way to impress Cornell and to hell with the case. She liked him; much more than she should. There, she had admitted it to herself, and she felt slightly better for doing so. It left her, however, in a very unprofessional position.

She sighed deeply, then picked up the phone and dialled Hanshaw's mobile number. There was no point in putting the inevitable off any longer. She had to report in sometime.

'Yes?' The voice on the other end of the call was gruff, irritated and too loud. Very much Derek Hanshaw, who hated modern gadgetry.

'Sam.'

'About bloody time. What have you been doing for the last fortnight?'

'Exactly what you told me to; getting myself into the good graces of our mutual friend.'

'You could have kept me posted.'

'Why. What have you found?' Her guts tied into a frozen knot.

'That's the bloody problem,' Hanshaw growled. 'Fuck all. He's either squeaky clean or very, very good at covering his tracks. Please tell me you've got something.'

'Sorry, Derek. Same story. He's polite and a gentleman. Okay, he's got an eye for the ladies, especially the younger ones, but he keeps it legal and above board. Even uses condoms, for Christ's sake.'

'Too much detail, Sam. Way too much. So what the fuck else have you been doing with your time. You moonlighting on me?'

'Why would I do that? You think maybe you don't

pay me enough?'

'Some people are greedy *and* stupid. Look, Sam, you were supposed to be digging up dirt on this guy at a personal level. You can't do that by going to the pictures and tea room dances. I know I asked you a lot but you could at least try.'

'I slept with him last night, Hanshaw.' Sam kept her voice flat, slightly tense. 'Do you need to know how many times?' It hurt her to tell Hanshaw and made her feel cheap.

There was a long silence from the phone. 'Sorry. I should have known better than to ...'

'Don't worry about it,' Sam interrupted, surprised by how much hostility had crept into her voice. 'It's what you're paying me to do.'

'It's so damned frustrating. I can't get anything worse than traffic offences on this man.'

'Perhaps that should tell you something, Hanshaw. Ever thought we could be shooting ourselves in the foot?'

'You know the rules. We aren't the cops. We don't do fair. We're just doing a job for a client.'

'I know, Derek, I know. Look, if it will make you feel any better, I'm going to be with him on Wednesday, and hopefully at the weekend. I'll try to have a snoop around his house while I'm there. Maybe I'll pick something up.'

'Let me know if you need anything. And watch your back.'

Sam disconnected the call, returned the wine glass to the kitchen and tried to find something to take her mind off the fact that she felt like a whore.

8

Hanshaw was in a foul mood. It wasn't easy to discern the difference between his normal grumpiness and his current state, but a trained eye would have spotted it. Nothing put his nose out of joint more than being on the wrong side in a fight, and the news Sam had given him on Sunday left him with a feeling that the entire Cornell case was going pear shaped in front of him.

The lack of evidence against Cornell was disturbing. He was honest in business, respected even. His record was clean. There were no irregularities with his banking arrangements, and Hanshaw would have bet money that the discrete call he had put in to a friend in HMRC was going to come back negative too. Nothing. He had been in the business long enough to know when things were being hidden from him, and also when he was being fed a line of bullshit. Nothing here was making his nose twitch. It really was beginning to look as though Cornell had nothing to hide.

Which led him to an interesting point. Cornell might have nothing to hide, but whoever it was wanted him out of the way certainly did. Why else was that snooty little mouse being sent to arrange payments and get reports instead of the client making personal visits? The insistence on cash payments meant the client didn't want anything recorded, either. The client was being a damn sight less honest than his supposed target. He threw his mind back three weeks to when he had been given the job, looking for more stuff that didn't add up.

The girl had not made an appointment. She had just walked in off the street and asked to see him. He remembered thinking she had looked odd when she was shown into his office. She had carried herself strangely, with a kind of rigid poise, as she walked over to his desk. He had noticed that she wore absurdly high heels. She had even looked unnatural when she had lowered herself so carefully into the chair, as though something was holding her spine straight.

She had got straight to the point; she was an agent for somebody else who wanted a man investigated with a view to removing him from his job. The man was a known womaniser, so a honey trap was indicated. He'd instantly recommended Sam. The girl had insisted they arrange an interview for Sam, to which he had reluctantly agreed, and after they had negotiated terms – which had been absurdly generous – the girl had left.

He had to admit it was odd. He'd seen weirder things in the 15 years he had been in the business, but this was close to the top of the list. And now it was Monday again, he had another negative report to deliver, and he was beginning to get uncomfortable. He chewed on his thumbnail; his teeth were too weak actually to bite anything off, but it was his cigar surrogate when he was in the office and people could be watching.

'Fuck it,' he muttered, and reached out to the button on the intercom. 'Joy? Is Tony still in the building?'

'No, Mr Hanshaw. In fact, I haven't seen him this morning.'

'Try his mobile. I want him here before 11.'

'I'll see what I can do.'

Hanshaw released the intercom and slouched back in his chair. He had an hour before the girl turned up for her report.

'My client has given me strict instructions,' she announced, trying to sound imperious and failing dismally. Hanshaw had guessed her to be about Sam's age the first time he had seen her, but today he revised his estimate down from 25 to about 20. When he had said there was still no news he was sure he had seen her face pale and take on an expression of panic for a second.

'Which are?' Hanshaw asked, trying to sound polite.

'If the report is still negative, which it is, I am to express my client's extreme displeasure. I am to remind you that there are many other agencies my client could approach. Finally, I am to suggest that unless some positive progress is made in the next two weeks, my client will take her business elsewhere.'

'And if there is nothing for us to find?'

The girl said nothing, just looked fixedly at a point slightly above Hanshaw's head. He waited a moment to make sure she had nothing more to say, then decided it was time to close the meeting. 'Whatever. Tell your client that the threat has been delivered and that I will continue to do my utmost, as always, to find a satisfactory answer.'

The girl got up to leave. Hanshaw followed her to

the door and held it open for her, but there were no goodbyes. He then hurried across to the window, peered down at the street and watched as the girl made her way to her parked car, got in and drove off. A few moments later, a trials bike farted past in the same direction.

Tony Ferrioni liked off-roaders. The high seat meant you could see three or four cars ahead. So the exhaust was naff, but they could go anywhere. Made tailing somebody easy, especially if they weren't a pro. This one definitely wasn't. He could have sat behind her in a bright pink Cadillac and she still wouldn't have guessed she was being followed.

He tailed her along the A10, then into Enfield. The traffic was almost gridlocked, and that was a problem. A bike sitting in a traffic jam was unnatural, too much of an eye-catcher. Still, he was familiar with this route, and knew there was only one way the girl could go for a few hundred yards yet. He wove through the creeping traffic and pulled over where he could see if she was taking any side roads. Putting the bike up on its stand, he pretended to fiddle with something on his back wheel.

It took two more fake breakdowns before she made enough progress that Tony could watch her turn off the one-way system into the car park of a medium-sized office unit. The unit was two floors tall and had 50 or so parking spaces. Tony waited a few minutes before he dug his mobile out of his jacket.

'Boss? Tony.'

'Well?'

'The fox just went to ground.'

'This isn't a fucking spy movie.'

'Offices in Enfield. Middlesex Street.'

'Name on the building?'

'Just letters. SCCS.'

'Say again?'

'Big blue letters. SCCS.' Tony waited, but there was only silence from the other end of the call. 'What should I do, boss?'

The eerie silence persisted for another ten or 15 seconds before Hanshaw growled his directions. 'Stay with it. I want to know where she goes next.'

Tony closed the connection and sighed. He liked to prepare for surveillance work, and hated being dropped in the deep end without warning. Still, improvisation was one of the things he was good at, or that's what he told everybody. He lifted the saddle from his bike, disconnected a reasonably important wire, and put the saddle back. There was a bench nearby with a good view, and his 'engine problems' gave him a reasonable excuse if anybody challenged him.

Hours passed uneventfully, and at a quarter to five Tony 'repaired' his bike. Fifteen minutes later his target reappeared, heading back into the town and heavy traffic. With the bike now 'fixed', Tony followed, almost losing the woman at a red light when she turned north up the Ridgeway. For a moment he thought about running the light as she slipped out of view, but there were signs saying the junction had cameras on it. Hanshaw would pay the fine but couldn't make the points go away. When the lights changed he rode like a courier with a nose full of Columbia's best until he caught up with her.

This time the girl seemed to be making some basic attempt to throw off a tail, or at least satisfy herself that no-one was doing so. She wound through the side roads of Gordon Hill, twice doing four right turns to see if someone was following. But Tony had too much experience and knew the area well enough to keep her in view while keeping himself out of sight. He continued right up to the point when she turned into the drive of a house in Botany Bay. He then pulled over a little way further down the road, so that the drive was still just in sight, and kept watch for her to come out again while he made another call.

'She's *where*?' Hanshaw barked.

'A fuck-off rich mansion in Botany Bay.'

'That makes no sense. She doesn't have that sort of money, or she wouldn't be doing this courier shit.'

'Gets better, boss. She went right around the houses to get there. Took 45 minutes to do a trip she could have done in 20. Couldn't have fooled anybody who was half-way serious.'

'But trying to hide it anyway,' Hanshaw mused. 'Can you cover the place?'

'Not easy, boss. And not tonight. Might be able to do something, but it won't be round-the-clock.'

'When?'

'Day after tomorrow.'

'Damn.' Hanshaw paused for a moment. 'All right. Do what you can. But make it quick.'

At 8.00 am on Wednesday morning a grey van pulled up opposite the house in Botany Bay. Stickers in the front and rear windows announced it was 'On Hire for Cabletech'. A man in overalls and a hard hat emerged from the vehicle, retrieved a toolkit from the back and squatted down behind the roadside cabinet that just happened to give a view along the drive of a certain large house.

Tony looked at the mess of wiring inside the cabinet and wondered how anybody ever made sense of it. To him it just looked like spaghetti, not nice and neat like his network cabling. Still, it wasn't as though he was going to touch anything. Much. He sat on his toolbox and pretended to be fascinated by the interior of the cabinet.

9

Sam had spent most of the week trying to occupy herself in some useful way, but had failed dismally and passed most of the time brooding. By Wednesday she had almost talked herself into ringing Cornell to cancel their evening, and probably would have done so if she had actually had a contact number for him.

Monday and Wednesday were usually exercise nights for her; Monday was Kendo, Wednesday ballet. Focusing hard on something else always seemed to clear her thoughts. But this Monday her sparring partner had handed Sam her ass on a plate and she had picked up a bruise on her arm despite the padding. She had even been to the pool twice over the last few days, but it seemed that no amount of swimming or being whacked with a bamboo pole was going to help clear her head.

The ballet classes were not particularly serious but she loved them. Control and poise, strength and suppleness. The group was relaxed and they had a laugh. She figured she still had time to attend this week's. Simon wasn't going to pick her up until 7.30 – she could get back and have a shower before he arrived. But the lesson was not a success. Sam couldn't focus. All she could think of was how unhappy she was about the situation she was in, and how much she was both dreading and longing for the weekend. She was so distracted that she earned a sharp word from the instructor as she left. Sam just nodded and avoided an argument. All she wanted was to get home and get ready, so she just pulled on her tracksuit and headed for the door.

When she got back to the flat, she saw that somebody had stolen her parking space, and she cursed loudly before realising that the car was Simon's. The swearing changed to a groan. He was early, and she was hardly in a fit state for visitors. She pasted on a smile as Simon got out of his car.

'Sorry,' he explained. 'The traffic wasn't as bad as I expected.'

Sam mumbled something and invited him in, kicking her trainers off as she walked through the front door and scooting them to the side.

'Have I put my foot in it?' he asked once they were indoors.

'What? Why?' Sam looked around the lounge and realised that she hadn't planned for him to actually come in. Airing clothes were draped over the backs of chairs, and an untidy pile of magazines threatened to tumble from the sofa.

'You seem a little … tense?'

Sam glared at him, then realised he was right – and it was his fault. She took a deep breath, held it, and let it slowly out. 'Sorry. I wasn't expecting you just yet. I thought I had time for a shower and that I wouldn't need to tidy in here.'

'Where have you been?'

'Ba … to the gym.' She flopped down on the sofa,

causing a waterfall of magazines to cascade to the floor. It took her another moment to realise he was still staring at her feet. 'What's the matter?' she asked as she drew them protectively closer.

'I'd love to know what gym you go to.'

'Why?'

'Do they all dress in thick white tights? With a seam? I warned you I have a thing about feet.'

'Oh. I forgot.' Sam felt her cheeks tingle.

'Show me what you're wearing.'

Something told Sam it might not be such a good idea. She wanted to plead that she was dirty and sweaty, and that she desperately needed a shower. She did not feel in the mood to be mocked; and who would do anything but sneer at a 25-year-old woman pretending to be a dancer?

But the expression on Cornell's face suggested she didn't really have much choice. He looked like a hungry Rottweiler in a butcher's shop. If she disappointed him in this, it might ruin everything she had spent so long setting up. 'You're going to insist?'

He nodded.

'All right. Eyes closed and no peeking.'

Cornell covered his eyes solemnly, no trace of a smile on his lips. Sam quickly pulled off her tracksuit and threw it onto the couch. Beneath she was wearing a regulation black leotard with scooped neck and long sleeves. Her tights were regulation white. Wrapped around her waist was a short chiffon skirt. She hadn't really intended it, but she found herself taking up a weird compromise between first and third positions.

'Can I open my eyes yet?' Cornell asked.

Sam ached to say no, but realised she was delaying the inevitable. 'If you like.'

Cornell took his hands down from his face and his eyes seemed to keep opening forever. She braced herself for the humouring smirk, but all she saw was a strange hunger in his eyes. 'You dance? Ballet?'

'More like an exercise class.'

'Why didn't you just tell me? Why all the secrecy?'

'I thought you'd laugh at me.'

'Why?'

'I don't exactly look the part.'

'You look close enough to me. May I see your shoes?'

'Eh?'

'I'd like to see the shoes you dance in.'

'They're old and disgusting and they smell.'

Cornell said nothing, but held out his hands. Sam shrugged and went to her kit bag. She handed him her battered Bloch point shoes, with darning over the box and holes worn in the lining at the heel.

'They're still warm,' he said. 'You dance *en pointe*?'

'Not very well.' She held her hands out to take the shoes back.

'Put them on.'

'Oh Simon, no.'

'Please.'

'Simon, I stink, so do these. I really want a shower. Why?'

'I said I had a thing about feet,' he said, eventually.

Sam considered for a moment and had to admit there was something interesting in the thought she might have something else she could use to manipulate him. 'I'll make you a deal.'

'I'm listening.'

'You let me go and shower, and I'll bring some of my dance stuff with me. I'll even try and dance for you if you can put up with me.'

'Tempting.'

'Honestly, I don't think you could turn me on now if you tried.'

He gave her a mischievous grin. 'Tempting, but not enough. Besides, I'm the one that's turned on and I think you need to do something about it before we go out. Sit on the couch.'

Cornell stood in front of her and loosened his belt. Sam swallowed hard. This seemed to be going in a direction she wasn't happy with, and she started to look for a way to say no without upsetting him. He saved her the trouble, pushing her backwards so she slouched in on the cushion, her ass almost hanging over the end. Whatever he had in mind didn't involve a blowjob, and for that she was grateful. Cornell slid his trousers and pants down his thighs. He was already semi-erect, and Sam wondered what the hell he had in mind this time.

He leaned forward, put his hands under her knees, and lifted them. Sam went along with the motion, pulling her feet up until they rested on the edge of the cushion. Cornell reached forward again, this time taking her ankles, and Sam finally realised what he was doing. She stifled a giggle and tried to keep a straight face as she realised he wanted her to use her feet to pleasure him. He really did have a thing about feet.

She placed her feet on either side of his prick and tried to stroke them back and forth. She stopped when he winced. Obviously she was doing something wrong, but she wasn't sure what. 'You'd better use your hands,' she said. 'I wouldn't want to break it off.'

Cornell put his hands on her feet and eased them back and forth along his cock. Sam turned her feet inwards, sole to sole, opening her legs wider. Cornell seemed to like the new position; his eyes closed and his face filled with intense concentration. It felt very strange at first, but then Sam realised it was no more than she had done when she had woken him after their first night together. She reached between her legs to add some enjoyment for herself, only to find that the leotard and the tights together were so thick that they robbed her of any sensation.

Cornell was fucking her feet now. He gave one soft moan, then started to come. His first jet of sperm almost reached her face, the rest pooled on her stomach. Cornell gave a final shudder, then seemed to pause for a moment before pulling himself upright and drawing in a deep breath. His eyes opened and his smile shone down on her.

'Mind if I sneak into the bathroom before you shower?'

For Tony, Wednesday was a waste of time. Two cars left the house in the morning, two returned in the evening. One he recognised as belonging to the mousy little girl, the other was an Audi Q series driven by an older woman. He guessed the latter was in her forties. She was smartly dressed and had full, dark hair.

Thursday seemed no better; both cars went out and returned just ten minutes apart, around the same time as they had the previous day. Tony made a note in his voice recorder but didn't get too excited until a third car turned up; a battered old Escort that looked like it hadn't seen an honest MOT for years. He quickly dictated the registration number into his recorder as he shifted sideways for a better view. The scruffily-dressed driver had his back to him as he levered his podgy body out of the car, so Tony couldn't get a clear look. But he did get an unobstructed view of the front door as someone opened it from the inside, and his eyes nearly bugged out of his head. It was the mousy little girl, but she looked like she was wearing some kind of maid's outfit. It was quite a distance away, but he was sure he saw stocking tops peeking out from under a very short skirt. He decided not to report that bit back to Hanshaw.

An hour later the door opened again. The scruff came out, face like thunder, and stormed to his car. For just a second, Tony felt the guy look at him. It was a glance held just too long, but then the man was in his car and spitting gravel up the side of the Audi as he spun his wheels, first to reverse, then to shoot forward towards the gate. As the Escort waited for a gap in the evening rush, Tony again felt eyes on him. Had he been made? What would have given him away? Working too late? The Escort screeched out into traffic with a howl of abused engine and battered clutch, and Tony brushed the feeling away as stakeout nerves.

Friday morning saw Tony set up just as he had done for the last two mornings. He watched the two cars pull away, then settled down to a boring day. There ought to be a way to use all this damned technology in the cabinet, he thought. Some way to use it to run a camera, or something. It might be April, but it was still cold, the wind howled down the road like it was in a hurry to get somewhere warmer, and his kidneys were taking a battering.

A white Transit pulled up, bumping onto the grass kerb and coming to a halt behind his grey van. He groaned as soon as he saw who was driving, and started to pack up his things. The passenger door of the van slammed. The driver stayed inside, watching the road.

'Well, well, if it's not Tony the ice cream man,' said the passenger, heading toward him.

'Don't you figure its time you came up with a new punchline?' said Tony, not looking up. 'I'd have thought you could have got someone to invent you a new one by now, Walker.'

'I like this one. You were leaving, weren't you?'

Tony gestured at his closed toolbox and the now-locked cabinet.

'Tasty. And you weren't thinking of coming back, were you? Only we spoke with the phone people and they said they would be sending someone round to check the box.'

'Thanks for the warning.' Tony knew perfectly well that Walker wouldn't have checked with anybody. He was muscle, nothing more, and that was all he had between the ears too.

'No worries. I had to deliver a message, anyway.' All the banter dropped out of Walker's voice. 'Tell whoever you're working for to keep their noses away from here.' Walker jerked his chin toward the house. 'Otherwise they'll get themselves involved in an accident.'

Tony nodded, keeping his contempt for the clumsy threat off his face, and watched as Walker got back into the white Transit. His driver sped off in a spray of wet earth and, a few moments later, Tony did the same.

Hanshaw was pacing around his living room. He had, unusually for him, knocked off early from the office and gone home. It was Friday, he was the boss, and so he figured he could do what he damn well pleased. The Cornell case was giving him an ulcer; at least, that was what it felt like. He couldn't remember another case that had got him so twisted up or left him with such a feeling that he wasn't in control of things. His mood hadn't been helped by Tony Ferrioni's report on Monday that he had tailed the strange girl who claimed to be representing his client back to the offices of SCCS – Simon Cornell's company. He hadn't expected that. Hanshaw hated surprises, and he hated to be wrong. The girl's destination smacked of an inside job, and he hated inside jobs. They usually turned out to be bad attacks of office politics, and he hated any kind of politics.

The fact that the girl was staying in a flash mansion in an area where she clearly didn't belong was just adding insult to injury. She surely wouldn't be able afford to rent a shed in that neck of the woods. He could tell she hadn't been born into money. What was she doing there? And who was the older woman Tony had seen at the house, keeping a similar routine? Could that be his mysterious client? The same woman who had 'vetted' Sam?

A phone call had instituted a search on the house. All he had wanted were the basic details; who owned it and who lived there. The reply had eventually been e-mailed to him that afternoon, and had soured his digestion still further.

He fixed himself a wine-sized glass of port, went over to the old oak dining table that doubled as a desk and read the reply again. It still said the house was owned by a US-based corporation and was being rented out to a tenant about whom no information could be found.

His mind flashed back to the last time he had spoken with Sam, and to the way she had been almost defending Cornell. It was beginning to look as though he might need to start paying attention to what she had said. Information on Cornell was plentiful and clean. There was no hint of a snow job. Shit, the man did not even try to hide the fact he had the sex drive of a rabbit on whiz. Hanshaw had figured Sam had become too involved with this Cornell, making her unreliable, but this new information cast a different light on things.

Why was his client trying to get rid of Cornell by digging up dirt on him? If the money she was pouring into Hanshaw's coffers was any indication of her disposable income, she could have just bought the guy out. Everybody had a price. There was something so wrong about that it made his teeth itch.

And just why was his client – or perhaps someone she was associated with – renting that house in Botany Bay? Rich people did not waste money, or they didn't stay rich for long. The rent on a house that size must have been bleeding her, or them, dry. For anything more than six months it would have been cheaper to buy the place and re-sell it. Unless they didn't want to worry about the disposal of an inconveniently large asset. Or unless they thought they might want to leave in a hurry.

It was all sufficiently suspicious to make Hanshaw want to dig a little deeper. He was a generally gruff and cold-seeming man, but underneath he had a solid sense of fairness. In the deepest part of his soul, the part that came out only during the second bottle of port, was a fierce pride that he had never knowingly helped the bad guys beat up on the good guys. He had no intention of making that mistake here. The doorbell rang just as he was making a mental note to call a few more useful people after the weekend.

Muttering something unpleasant under his breath he put his empty glass on the table and made his way to the door. The bell rang twice more before he got there, ensuring the visitor would get a frosty reception. He reached up with a hand and twisted the lever of the cylinder lock.

The door burst inwards so violently that it could only have been kicked. Hanshaw was thrown back into the room as the door crashed first into his wrist, then into his shoulder. He fell heavily as his feet tangled under him, and a stabbing pain in his wrist got much, much worse as he used that hand to break his fall. He shook his head to clear it, and when his eyes drifted back into focus he found himself staring up at someone he recognised.

'Walker. David Walker, you fucking arse.'

The cocksure grin on the unwelcome visitor's face faded slightly. 'What of it?'

'What the fuck do you think you're playing at?' Hanshaw shouted, scrambling to his feet.

'Shut up, you old fart. I've got a message for you.' Walker strolled further into the room, followed by another side of beef who quietly closed the door. Walker looked around the living room and sneered. 'I always figured you for a stingy git from the way you dress, but I never put you down for a miser. Have you ever spent a penny on this gaff?'

'Don't give me that East End tough guy bollocks. I used to eat little shits like you for breakfast when you were still crapping your pants.'

Walker backhanded Hanshaw across the face, hard. Hanshaw didn't go down, quite, but he had to support himself by holding onto the dining table with his uninjured hand. He hadn't been prepared for the blow or its savagery. He decided to stay out of reach when he saw the look in Walker's eyes.

'I told you to shut your mouth. I've got a message to deliver, but nobody said how I had to deliver it.'

Hanshaw didn't move, although he was aware of the other muscle easing around the table behind him. Walker had a bad name. Hanshaw had bumped into him four years earlier, then working as a bodyguard for a mouthy little pimp in Southwark. Word had it that he took a little too much pleasure in his work, especially bringing the girls back into line, and had a nasty habit of improvising.

'So talk to me,' said Hanshaw.

'No rush,' said Walker, the cocky grin back to full strength. 'Don't you offer your guests a drink when they come to visit?'

'I've got whiskey or port.'

'My, my. Port. Aren't we posh? Whiskey'll be fine.'

Hanshaw went over to the side table. Walker followed and snatched the bottle from his hand before Hanshaw could find a glass.

'No point making washing up,' said Walker, throwing away the twist cap and taking a long pull at the whiskey. He belched loudly as he lowered the bottle from his lips.

'You've been naughty, old man.'

At 52, Hanshaw did not consider himself old, and normally took exception to the appellation. On this occasion he held his tongue and waited as Walker took another pull from the whiskey. Bullies were always more dangerous when they were drunk. Walker waved the bottle towards his colleague, but the man shook his head. Hanshaw thought he saw a glimmer of contempt, too. At least the other man was more professional than Walker. Hopefully this wouldn't get out of hand.

'Have I?' he asked, in response to Walker's

statement.

'You have. Somebody is very cross with you.'

'Who's that?'

'A person who is paying you a large amount of money, yet you seem to be spending a lot of time poking into their business instead of doing your job.'

'Ah. Our Lady of Botany Bay.'

The smile slipped again. 'Very clever, old man, but you had better leave it at that. Your client doesn't appreciate … disloyalty.' Walker had a little trouble with the word. Hanshaw couldn't tell if it was because of the drink, or because 'loyalty' wasn't a word that fit well in Walker's mouth. 'Your client asked me to pass on a warning that if you don't keep your nose out of her business, it's likely to get broken.'

'Is that it?'

Walker took another swig of the whiskey and Hanshaw winced at his cavalier treatment of the 20-year-old Islay malt. 'Maybe. Like I told you, nobody said how the message was to be delivered.'

'Give over, Walker. You've done your job.'

'But I have to make sure you believe me.'

A nugget of fear began to grow in Hanshaw's gut. Ten years earlier, Walker would not have been a problem. If things turned nasty now, Hanshaw was in for a hiding. Walker struggled to pull something bulky out of his coat pocket. Hanshaw took a moment to recognise it as a roll of duct tape, and he groaned inwardly.

'Stand up, granddad, and stick your hands out.'

'Ah, leave it out –'

The whiskey bottle thumped down onto the table and Hanshaw watched it wobble. His eyes returned to Walker and found a five inch blade had appeared in the thug's other hand.

'Stop pushing me, old man. Put your fucking hands out. Now.'

Hanshaw did as he was told. Walker put the knife between his teeth then started to wrap tape around the older man's wrists. Another strip pinioned his upper arms, and finally a strip was fixed across his mouth. Walker prodded Hanshaw with the blade.

'Upstairs. Wouldn't want to have to leave you on the floor, would we.'

Hanshaw went up to his bedroom. Walker pushed him onto his bed, then used more tape around his ankles and knees. Hanshaw kept calm, outside, and did what he was told. Inside, he was terrified. Walker could leave him for days before he told anybody what he'd done. Or, knowing Walker, he might decide not to tell anybody at all and leave him to die. He'd be barely able to move the way Walker had trussed him, and his mobile was on the kitchen worktop. If Walker lived up to his reputation, Hanshaw's only hope would be that someone came looking for him, and rescued him if they were in time. He could feel the sweat of oncoming panic trickling down the side of his face, but tried to convince himself that being left like this would at least be better than antagonising Walker and getting a knife in his kidney.

A last strip of tape went over Handsaw's eyes and Walker stepped back from the bed, laughing as he admired his handiwork. 'That should keep you quiet, granddad. Give you plenty of time to think on the message, eh?' He grabbed Hanshaw's face with one hand, pressing fingers and thumb into his cheeks. 'Hope you have good friends, or they'll only find you when your neighbours complain about the smell.' He gave Hanshaw's head a savage shake and let go.

As Walker and his helper walked out, Hanshaw listened to their footsteps receding down the stairs. A moment later the front door slammed shut. Hanshaw was grateful that at least the fuckwit hadn't left it open for any of his mates to come back later and gut the place. His right wrist was on fire; sprained or maybe even broken. He stretched as best he could, trying to make himself comfortable. He might be in for a long wait.

10

'All right, tonight we stay in. Just don't forget the other half of the deal,' said Sam

'What?'

'I get to look in the other wardrobe.'

'And just when did I agree to that?'

'I just decided.'

Cornell shook his head. 'You are incorrigible. Perhaps. Bribe me.'

'Oh, I intend to, but I just wanted to make sure we knew what the stakes were in advance.'

It was Saturday. The plan had originally been that Cornell would pick Sam up at six, then they would go out for a meal before heading back to his place. However, having got Simon's mobile number from him on Wednesday evening, Sam had phoned on Thursday and changed the agenda. She had made her own way to Harlow and had taken a cab from there. Now it was five in the afternoon and she was negotiating with Simon about how the rest of the evening would go.

'Anything else?' he asked.

'Yes. I need plenty of space in here. Oh, and put one of the dining chairs in the middle of the room. You should slip into something more comfortable, like a robe, and be sitting in the chair by the time I'm ready.'

Cornell started pushing furniture out of the way and caught a glimpse of Sam putting a disc into the CD player before she disappeared in the general direction of the bedrooms. As soon as he was done, he went to get ready. As he stood naked in his bedroom, he decided he must have died and gone to heaven. Nobody deserved to have this much luck in one lifetime. Meeting Sam had been good enough to make any man give thanks for his karma, but this was just cherry on the icing. A plethora of possibilities flashed through his mind, but he pushed them all aside. For now. Sam still had to be nurtured and treated with a respect he didn't normally bother with. She was enthusiastic, and inquisitive enough. All he needed to do was guide her; just a gentle nudge here and there, and allow her to think she had found her own way to what he ultimately desired.

He slipped into his robe and felt something in the pocket tap against his hip. He took it out and smiled; a spare condom from the previous weekend had managed to stay put during the wash. How appropriate. He put it back and returned to the lounge. Sam had not yet put in an appearance, so he positioned one of the chairs as she had asked and found himself somewhere to sit on a couch that offered a good view. He noticed that the remote for the CD player was missing, and guessed that Sam must have taken it.

His guess was right. Not long after he had settled himself, the unfamiliar strains of Gershwin's 'Rhapsody in Blue' wailed from the speakers and Sam entered from the hallway.

A leg entered first, clad in something opaque and white and shod in a red *pointe* shoe laced tightly around her ankle. The rest of her followed the leg, sliding sinuously around the corner. Cornell stopped breathing for a moment. The leg-wear was either a long sock or a hold-up. Above that she had on a short dress of brilliant red with spaghetti straps and a back so low it almost reached her ass. The material was thin and clung to her like silk, hiding nothing of her nipples as they pressed firmly against it. The skirt looked flimsy enough to fly up at the slightest provocation.

Sam turned her back to the wall and he saw she had been at the make-up too; dark eye shadow and bright red lipstick. She looked at him with her eyes half closed, lips parted, then slowly ran her tongue across the vivid red. Her feet were turned out so far they almost touched the wall, and she slowly eased them sideways until they were level with her shoulders, all the while running her hands over her arms and neck. As she brought her hands down to her breasts, she slid down the wall into a perverted *plié*. Her legs were spread so wide that her knees almost touched the walls too, and only a flap of the skirt covered her sex. She teased her nipples, then eased a hand down to her thighs and along to the hem of the skirt. Slowly, taunting him, she lifted it.

His already erect cock spasmed. She had shaved herself, and he could see the delicate edges of her inner labia peeking through the outer lips of her vagina, spread obscenely by her position. He almost came as she slowly ran her middle finger through her sex then placed it deep into her mouth. She slid back up the wall, onto *pointe*, and began to dance.

It could not have been considered choreographed, even by the most generous of observers. She caressed her body continuously as she danced around the chair in the middle of the room, using it as a prop, taking every opportunity she could to show him a pointed foot or a flash of her bare pussy. She made a great show of teasing her nipples through the thin material of the dress, even pinching them.

Cornell was mesmerised. At the start of the dance he had undone the robe with the intention of masturbating while he watched, but he kept his hands firmly on his thighs. The sexuality of her dance had stunned him, and he knew if he touched himself he would ejaculate.

Sam came to him, taking his hands and pulling him up from the couch. She led him to the chair she had used so much during her dance and pushed him into it. He fell heavily and his robe dropped open. Sam stepped back, went up *en pointe* and walked towards him again. She placed her legs on either side of his, her breasts thrust into his face, then slowly and deliberately lowered herself onto his prick. As he slid inside her, she gasped out, then paused for a moment with her hands on his shoulders until she had steadied herself. She started to ride him. The motion was slightly unusual, and it took Cornell a moment to realise that Sam was still *en pointe*.

She set up a hard, fast rhythm, lifting herself until he was only just inside, then impaling herself again. Each time she dropped herself down his shaft she left out a grunt. At first Cornell put his hands on her waist to steady her but, when he was sure she had her balance, he felt free to indulge himself with her breasts. Touching them through the soft fabric was nice enough, but Cornell felt her skin was softer still. Besides, her arms kept getting in the way.

He took her hands from his shoulders and held them at her side for a moment, then reached up and flicked the straps off her shoulders. Sam pulled her arms free and put them back on Cornell's shoulders. He was just about to push them down to her sides again when the straps gave him an idea. He guided her hands to the small of her back and looped the string straps around them. Secure it was not, but the symbolism was there, and as he pulled the knot tight Sam arched her back and moaned.

Cornell took this as a sign of approval and put his hands back on Sam's waist, using them to add a little of his own downward momentum to each of her thrusts. The added effort seemed to push her that little bit closer to the edge. She began to pant and her head began to loll from side to side. It took Cornell a moment to realise that the pants had words in them, punched out with each downward thrust.

'Nip … ples … pinch … ni …'

Cornell took each hard bud between a finger and thumb.

'Fuck. Yes', Sam moaned. 'Harder.'

Cornell was surprised, as he wasn't being exactly gentle. He added pressure and introduced a twist. Sam let out a loud cry and came almost instantly.

Cornell did not. He had every intention of drawing this out as long as he could, and of making a point. Sam had collapsed forward onto his chest, but he gave her no time to recover. 'Don't stop,' he said, a hard edge in his voice.

Sam lifted her face, groggy and confused.

'I said don't stop.'

'Simon, I can't …'

'Move it, bitch. Keep fucking yourself on my prick until I say you can stop.' He put his hands under her ribs and started to raise and lower her himself. A few seconds later, Sam half-heartedly joined in. 'Simon, I don't know ...'

He gently slapped her left breast; no more than a gentle swat and not hard enough to leave a mark, but enough to make her jump. 'Sluts don't stop until their masters tell them to. Now back on your toes and fuck yourself.'

It had been a gamble, but it appeared to pay off. Sam started to fuck him more enthusiastically, even if with a dazed look and slightly less co-ordination, but Cornell was even more aroused by the sight. He kept his hands where he could catch her if she slipped, and could just reach to flick her nipples with his thumbs. He was waiting for her eyes to glaze over again.

'Don't come,' he repeated. 'Don't come until I tell you to.'

'Please,' Sam moaned. 'I can't stop it.'

'Fight it.' Cornell swatted her on the behind.

Sam did not reply, but she caught her bottom lip between her teeth and screwed her eyes shut in concentration. Cornell could only watch her trying to hold back her orgasm for a few moments before he felt his start to build. He moved his hands down to her waist, set up his own more insistent rhythm, and forced her down harder onto his prick.

'Now,' he hissed. 'Come now.'

He felt the walls of her vagina spasm as the words left his mouth, clamping around his prick and milking him as she orgasmed. He ejaculated, explosively and seemingly forever. He felt tears spring into his eyes as he came.

Things went vague for a while. The next thing Cornell was fully aware of was a warm feeling of fulfilment and the dead weight of Sam on his lap and chest. He wondered if she had passed out until he heard her making a satisfied purr. He was still semi-erect inside her and briefly toyed with the idea of a repeat performance, then grinned and thought himself a greedy fool. He unlooped the shoulder straps and put his arms around Sam as he tried to keep her warm until she was ready to move.

Cornell held her a little tighter as she shivered. The first thing she said was 'Cold.' The second was 'Oh, you untied me.' He filed the comment, as well as the hint of disappointment, away for future reference. Cornell helped her stand then led her over to the couch and made her lie down before covering her with the robe he had been wearing. It wasn't much, but she would be comfortable. He wanted to bury his face between her legs and make her come again and again, but as a second best he padded into the kitchen in search of refreshment.

When Sam stirred she offered Cornell a sleepy smile as she sat up and pulled the straps of her dress back over her shoulders. She had dozed for been long enough for him to fetch a glass of wine, but other than that he had lost track of time as he had sat staring at her.

'Drink?' he offered.

She nodded. 'Juice, please. My mouth feels furry.'

He obliged, placing the glass on a table next to the couch and turning away. Sam grabbed hold of his arm.

'Why do you always sit half a room away from me?'

'So I can see you better.'

'Try sitting next to me for a change,' she suggested.

Cornell hesitated for a split second. He really would prefer to sit where he had the best view, but the fact that she had brought the matter up suggested it mattered to her. He sat next to her, expecting her to snuggle up to him. Instead she scooted down to the other end of the couch and sat facing him, cross legged. He had to admit that the view was better.

'How are you feeling?' he asked.

Sam gave him a warm smile. 'Absolutely marvellous. What about you.'

'Shell-shocked. That was not something the English National would be likely to choreograph.'

Sam uncrossed her legs and stretched them out. One foot settled in Cornell's lap, elegantly pointed. The other she used to rub the box of her shoe against one of his nipples. 'Why, whatever are you implying?'

'Nothing at all,' he said, grabbing her wandering foot and easing it down to join its partner. 'What would you like to do for the rest of the evening?'

'You have to ask? You promised.'

Cornell was confused for a moment, then the penny dropped. 'You can't be serious?'

'Why not?'

'You haven't had enough yet?'

A ballet shoe began to gently rub across his crotch. 'Why, have you? Did I wear you out?'

Cornell felt his prick begin to stir. 'A man could take that as an insult.'

'I'll take it as an insult if you don't keep your bargain.'

Cornell sighed and gently pushed Sam's foot away from his prick. The feel of her shoe in his hand momentarily aroused him further, but he pushed the thought from his mind. He had been dreading this moment, and had been hoping that Sam had forgotten about it. Now, it seemed as though he had little chance of talking her out of it.

'What's wrong,' asked Sam, all the playfulness gone from her voice, replaced by concern.

'I'm afraid, to be honest.'

'Of what?'

'Of you. Or rather, of what you might think.'

She looked hurt for a second, then thoughtful. 'Is what is in that wardrobe so terrible?'

'Not to me,' said Cornell, his eyes dropping to stare at the floor. 'Others could think differently. You might think differently.' He could not look at her. He knew he was hurting her, but couldn't help himself. He was firmly impaled on the horns of a first class dilemma. If he was to let her see his other collection, she might storm out of the house in disgust, and out of his life. It had happened before. Alternatively, if he left her ignorant, her unsatisfied curiosity and inevitable suspicion could drive a wedge between them just as damaging.

The sofa moved. Sam edged closer to him, then straddled across his thighs. Her hands took hold of his ears and gently twisted until he looked up and into her eyes, now only inches from his. 'You really have a problem with this, don't you?'

He nodded, as much as he could, and Sam shook her head. 'I wish I understood why. I wish I understood what it was you were afraid of.'

'Losing you.' As soon as the words blurted from his lips Cornell wished he'd bitten his tongue off instead. This was worse than anything else he could have said. He felt incredibly, horribly stupid, but it was the truth. He had probably done more to scare Sam off than if he had tried to turn her into a fetish diva on their first date. He wanted to crawl away into a dark hole and pull it in behind him. Sam's face had gone blank and rigid, as though she was trying to hide something. A pause hung in the air like some harbinger of impending doom and lasted seemingly for hours.

A lopsided smile crept slowly across Sam's lips, then she used his ears to shake his head from side to side. The experience was not painless. 'Oh no, Simon Cornell. That was a nice try, but no result. One, you are not going to get rid of me that easily. Two, you are not going to talk your way out of that promise. Would you like to apologise for insulting me now?'

'What insult?'

Her face shifted to a more serious expression. 'The one that implied I wasn't mature enough to take what I see at face value. The one that implied I was judgemental. The one that suggested I would run screaming into the night if I didn't like what I saw.'

'I apologise. Honestly. I never meant to insult you.'

She shut him up by kissing him, just a peck at first, but then her tongue began to demand access to his mouth and he responded instinctively, passionately.

'Now,' Sam sounded breathless when she finally pulled away. 'Shall we go?'

'Right now?'

'Right now.'

11

Tony Ferrioni was about to go out. He had a date; nothing important, just a pretty little thing he had picked up the night before in a pub in Tottenham. He figured he would impress her with a good restaurant then maybe get to screw her later. Before he left home he decided to try Hanshaw again. If the boss didn't need him for anything, he could at least get pissed if he didn't get laid, and he still hadn't had a chance to report his encounter with Dave Walker.

The phone rang and went to voicemail. Tony grimaced. Hanshaw rarely didn't answer. He left it five minutes then tried again. Voicemail. Tony tried the office. It was a long shot, but maybe Hanshaw's phone battery had died and he'd left his charger at work. Besides, this was the only other number Tony had. The call connected, but again only to an answering machine.

Tony felt uncomfortable. He had every intention of having a good time that night, or drowning his sorrows in style if things did not go according to plan. He did not want to be interrupted, or to have to work his way through a hangover in the morning. Hanshaw's place was more or less on his way to pick up his lady for the night, so he decided to drop by.

It was dusk when he pulled up outside Hanshaw's, a '30s semi, obviously inhabited by a confirmed bachelor. The ragged patch of grass at the front needed mowing and the shrubs in the border were almost half way up the window. There were no lights on anywhere, so far as Tony could see, but he got out of his car and walked up to the front door anyway. He rang the bell, then rang it again a minute later. No answer, and no sounds within when he pressed his ear to the door. When he pushed one of the shrubs aside and peered in through the window, all he could see were the net curtains, vague shapes and his reflection.

He'd done what he could, and he went back to his car. With the engine running, the gear engaged and the handbrake off, he still hesitated before driving away. Something didn't feel right. He shrugged, checked his mirror and pulled away. It would either come to him or it wouldn't, but he wasn't going to risk missing a shag sitting here waiting to figure out what it was.

Sam climbed off Cornell's lap, stood up and held out her hands. Cornell allowed her to pull him to his feet and lead him to the guest bedroom. An uncomfortable chill had settled just below his sternum despite Sam's assurances and he felt a frown cramping his forehead. Sam was rummaging in her bag, so he waited a moment to unlock the second door. He was about to pull it aside when Sam called 'Wait.'

He turned back to face her. She was seated on the end of the bed, untying the ribbons of her *pointe* shoes. He drew breath to object, but Sam wasn't looking at him and spoke first.

'Let me do it,' she said as she slipped the Blochs off her feet and threw them at her bag in the corner. They missed, and the hard boxes clattered against the floor. She picked up something that Cornell had not seen hidden behind her.

'I don't understand.'

Sam was pulling soft leather slippers onto her feet, just as red as the *pointe* shoes, and Cornell wasn't sure which he preferred. 'I don't want you to interfere. I want you to sit on the other side of the room, or on the bed, and just watch. I sort of have something I want to prove to you. I want to do this for myself, without you picking things out for me or steering me.'

Cornell understood. If she wanted a free rein, she could have it. In a way, he liked the idea. At least it would give him a more honest indication of what Sam found interesting. Assuming, of course, that she was being honest. He had a feeling she would be. 'Are you sure you want me to watch?'

'Oh, absolutely,' she replied with a curiously decisive tone. 'And I want you to keep quiet. Unless I ask a question, I don't want you to make a sound until I close the door.' She lifted a foot, arched it, and poked him in the leg. 'Now, out of the way.'

Sam stepped towards the door but hesitated for a moment. At first he wondered if she was having second thoughts, then he realised she was checking herself out in the mirror. Judging by the little smile toying with her lips, she liked what she saw. Then she reached out, took hold of the handle, and slid the door aside. She made no further move for half a minute, except for her hand falling limply to her side.

'My God.' Her voice was so quiet he barely heard it. He knew that as soon as she slid the door open she would be enfolded in an intense aroma, and it was probably that that had stopped her in her tracks. She stepped forward and lifted the hem of some anonymous garment. Her fingers stroked it, then she raised the material to her face and inhaled. She let go of the garment and turned to face him.

'This is all rubber.' It was more of a statement than a question.

'Mostly,' he agreed, keeping it short. 'Or leather.'

'Now this I *have* to try,' she said as she turned away, so softly he wasn't sure if he was even meant to hear, and it wasn't clear if she was meaning the collection in general or a specific item. 'Let's see what else is in here first.'

She had moved slightly to the side, giving him a better view of what she was doing, and he was pleased that she had remembered to include him in her examination. She worked her way along the rail like she was at a boutique, skipping quickly over some things, looking more closely at others. Cornell sat on the stool for the dressing table, heart hammering in his throat, caught between arousal and fear as she went from garment to garment, some plainly designed for restraint, and wondered if he had done the right thing. Should he have insisted on keeping control, on introducing her to the next stage – he hoped – of their relationship at a slower pace?

Sam turned her attention away from the rail to the built-in shelves and drawers. This was where Cornell kept the smaller items, and he held his breath as she pulled open the top one.

'First question,' she said without turning. 'Is this stuff for you, or do you expect me to wear it?'

That drawer was full of restraints; cuffs, collars,

gags, handcuffs and ropes. Cornell had been waiting for the question, and had worked out a reply. 'I don't *expect* you to wear anything, but being dominated does not interest me at all.'

'Thank God for that,' breathed Sam. 'I was worried you got off on being whipped by women.'

'No, I prefer to do the whipping myself.' He knew it was stepping outside the boundaries of silence Sam had requested, but she was the one making conversation. She looked over her shoulder at him.

'Is that a promise?'

'If you ask me nicely enough,' he replied, then waved her back to the wardrobe.

Sam poked her tongue out at him then turned back to the cupboard, shifting slightly so she blocked his view as she worked her way down the drawers. He could see she was holding some things up against her to check for size. Some were returned, others placed to one side, presumably for further examination later.

Cornell expected her to go back to the rail, but she slid the door closed and turned back to him. 'Don't worry, I haven't finished. I am absolutely parched. Any chance of a coffee?'

Cornell managed a non-committal shrug and said 'If you like'. The request seemed a little odd, and he wasn't sure he liked what he saw in Sam's eyes. Privately, he thought it more likely she needed some time without him watching her and didn't want to ask. That touched a sore spot; he would have preferred she just say. He rose from the stool, kissed her in passing, and headed for the kitchen – resolving not to hurry back.

Sam breathed out a huge sigh once Simon had left the

room. She hoped she hadn't been too transparent, but she needed some time away from him. It had been fairly obvious that this was the direction things were heading in, but now she was confronted with the reality … Was she actually afraid? And if so, why?

It wasn't that the contents of the cupboard didn't interest her, excite her, but the implications made her pause. Ignoring the clothing, there were things in there that would deprive her of her freedom, and by implication, of her will. Simon wasn't the sort of man to have these things just as glorified costume jewellery. At first, possibly, but not for her, not for someone who was as connected with him as she was. She could insist on restrictions, boundaries, but then the relationship would be artificial, pointless. Was that somewhere she wanted to go with him?

The professional in her clamoured for attention, pointing out that she didn't have much choice. She was still investigating him, and the job wasn't finished. If she didn't play the part, and play it convincingly, they would almost certainly drift apart and that wouldn't get the job done.

The woman in her said to hell with the job, think about the man. Nobody had ever managed to do this to her before. She had always thought herself to be independent and her own person, but Cornell was changing something in her. He was pushing her, making her extend herself in directions she had never imagined. What was worse, or better, was that he had been doing it so subtly that he, not she, had been making the decisions, guiding her actions. She was also beginning to realise that she could no longer bear to disappoint him, no matter how outrageous his demands became. The admission gave her a funny feeling in her chest; fluttery, and both warm and cold at the same time.

Sam stripped off and went back to the cupboard. There were some things she had thought might make a good place to start and she moved them to the bed. They looked simple enough; a wide suspender belt, a pair of stockings, and a pair of opera gloves – all black, all rubber. She held the gloves to her face, drawing the scent through her nose in a long breath. It made her feel light-headed; her nipples tightened immediately and her clit tingled. She drew them on, delighted to find they reached almost to her armpits. They were constrictive without being restrictive, and made subtle noises when she moved. She rubbed a thumb over a nipple and gasped at the unique sensation. She did it again, both nipples this time, then pinched them as hard as she thought Simon would, biting back the cry.

The thought of investigating him had begun to repel her, and smacked of betrayal. The only fly in the ointment was the tiny kernel of uncertainty she couldn't shake. Somebody was of the opinion that there was sufficient dirt on this man to go to the lengths of shelling out a great deal of money to have him exposed. The reason for this still had to be resolved.

She put on the suspender belt then slid her legs into the embrace of the stockings, making sure they were wrinkle-free before clipping on the suspenders. She hesitated a moment before putting her *pointe* shoes back on. She guessed Simon would be delighted with her feet as they were, rubber-clad, but decided to give him the choice. Perhaps he would enjoy taking them off.

In her heart she knew he was guilty of nothing more than a somewhat unconventional sexual appetite but, while she had learned to give her heart a fair hearing, it was Sam's nature to let her head rule. A compromise occurred to her: prove his innocence rather than his guilt. It would satisfy both her professional and personal sides, and it wouldn't really be cheating Hanshaw. Of course, she would still have to be discreet. Cornell was not entirely predictable, and she wasn't sure how he would react if he found out that she was, or had been, investigating him.

Sam picked up one of the last objects she had put on the bed. The collar was made of bright, shining metal, backed by soft leather. This was the choice. If she went out as she was, they were still playing dress up. Otherwise, she was telling Simon she was ready for him to lead her further down the path to … to where? The fastening on the collar was adjustable, but she couldn't make it stay shut. The same went for the cuffs. Disappointed, she took them back to the wardrobe, intending to look for something else. As she pulled the drawer out to put them away, Sam noticed a half-dozen small padlocks, also silver, rattling around in the bottom of the drawer. She held one up to the fastening of the collar, and felt another flutter in her stomach. So that was how they closed, and she couldn't see any keys.

She took everything back to the bed and started with her ankles, then her wrists. The padlocks felt heavy, intrusive, and incredibly real. The collar was either too loose, or slightly too tight. Breath coming too quickly and heart thumping in her ears, Sam pushed the padlock closed in the tighter position. As she heard, and felt, the lock click into place, Sam almost came. It was all she could do not to plunge her fingers into her sex, but that was Simon's decision now.

She slid the red dance dress over her head, settled it in place, then quickly touched up her hair and make-up before going to look for Simon.

13

Sam lay still for hours, breathing slowly and deeply and trying not to let the tension in her mind show in her body. They had not gone to bed until after midnight, and she wanted to make sure that Cornell was asleep before she made her move. When the clock beside the bed showed 02:00, she decided it was safe. Cornell should be at the bottom of a deep sleep cycle; his breathing was deep and regular and she would have sworn he was out cold. She slid out from under the light quilt, moving slowly, trying not to make the bed quake. For, she thought, a joke, Cornell had given her a pink teddy set – with matching booties – to wear to bed, but she still had on the rubber garments underneath and was afraid they might squeak if she moved too quickly.

Cornell did not stir and she crept out of the bedroom, leaving the door open in case the latch clicked when it closed. It seemed to take forever to creep along to Cornell's office, and she held her breath as she gently opened the door, praying to St Jude that neither the latch nor the hinges would chose this moment to develop a creak. The ambient light was barely enough for her to get around the room, and certainly not enough to investigate by. A torch would have been ideal, but she settled for pushing the door to, as she had the bedroom door, and clicking the switch on the banker's lamp on the edge of Cornell's desk.

She sat in his chair, settling gingerly, almost sighing as the cool of the leather penetrated her rubber knickers. Her backside was still tender from the paddling Cornell had given her, and her anus ached a little from being plugged for the first time – and yet she still felt a tingle of excitement in her sex as the discomfort triggered memories of the evening's events.

The drawers to the left were fakes and hid a small drinks cabinet. Sam was almost tempted to help herself to a shot. Her heart was racing and her hands felt clammy. She closed the cabinet; the sooner she finished here the sooner she could hurry back to bed and, if challenged, lie that she had only been going to the toilet. She felt she was betraying him even as she tried to help him, and at that moment she came close to simply going back to bed and resolving to tell him everything in the morning. She actually reached out to switch off the desk lamp, but then froze again. What if Cornell didn't believe her? What if he thought she was trying to set him up? She sat back in the chair and ran her hands through her hair. Every decision seemed to send her off into a twisting corridor of confusion and doubt.

She took a deep breath, held it, and let it slowly out. What was she thinking? She was an investigator. This was a job. Yes, there were personal elements, but the job came first. If she found what she expected, then no harm was done and she was in a better position to help him. If she found something wrong, then better she knew now.

On the right of the desk a large file drawer

dominated at the bottom, and two smaller drawers sat above. The top drawer contained just pens and paperclips, and she even lifted the tray out to make sure nothing was hidden beneath. The drawer below was full of larger stuff, including a stapler and a calculator, but the only paperwork she could find was a diary-cum-phonebook, bound in leather and with Cornell's name embossed across the top in gold lettering. She lifted it out and beneath it found a cheque book. Only two cheques had been used and neither stub had anything written on it. She jotted down the account details on a sticky note out of habit then flicked through the diary. It was empty apart from a couple of half-hearted entries in January. She guessed it had been an inappropriate gift. Simon would have everything on his laptop, or his Smartphone, and she knew her chances of getting access to either were minute. And in that moment she almost groaned out loud. Why hadn't she realised that sooner? This was pointless. There was no way she was going to find anything useful here, and she was risking everything. She had her hand on the drawer to close it when the office door opened and the main light flicked on.

'I can't wait to hear your explanation for this.'

Sam let her head sink to the desk. 'Fuck, fuck, bugger and fuck,' she muttered, then she sat up. 'Simon, it's not what you think.'

Cornell was stood on the other side of the desk, leaning forward on hands curled into fists, facing her. His expression was one of fury, but his eyes showed a hurt so profound that it ripped at her heart. 'I'm all ears.'

'Would you believe I was giving you an excuse to punish me later?' she tried to grin, to defuse the situation, but Cornell didn't move. 'All right, I'm a private investigator. I –'

'Bitch!'

'Simon, wait. Somebody is trying to dig up dirt on you. Somebody is trying to hurt you.'

'And you thought you'd help them.'

'Damn it, no. I mean, at first I was trying to do my job, yes, but not now.'

'Of course. And what was that job? Whoring to me so you could get in here and snoop around?'

'I've already told my boss he's after the wrong man. I was just looking for stuff to back that up. If I don't have anything concrete he won't believe me. I'm trying to help you, Simon. Please.'

'Of course you are,' Cornell's voice was heavy with sarcasm. 'Why didn't you just tell me all this?'

Sam drew breath to answer, but Cornell didn't give her a chance. 'I'll tell you why. Because you are a lying, two-faced whore. What was next, bitch? Back to your boss to give him all the lurid details? Hidden cameras so you can frame me for rape? Is that it?'

Sam wanted to die, right there and right then. Her own heart was being crushed in her chest and there was nothing she could do, because there was nothing she could say that he would believe. Even though she would have done anything for him, she still had to do her stupid job and mess everything up. Why should he believe her now? All he had was what his eyes were telling him. Add that to how quickly they had become so close, so open with each other, and how could he think it was anything but a contrivance on her part? She had to try one last time.

'What can I do to make you believe me?' Tears welled up as she spoke, and she dashed them angrily from her eyes. Why did she have to start crying now, at the exact moment when Simon would expect her to turn on the waterworks?

'Get your things and get out of my house. I'll call you a taxi.'

'Simon –'

'Shut up. If you aren't out of the house in five minutes I'll throw you out exactly how you are now.'

Sam got up from the desk and walked slowly past Simon. She paused at the door and looked back, hoping for an opportunity to make one more appeal. Cornell was still stood at the desk, head bowed and shoulders slumped, his back to her.

'Four minutes,' he said without looking up. Sam sighed and ran back to the guest room. She had no time to undress, but quickly pulled a blouse and jeans over the playsuit as she stuffed what she couldn't afford to leave into her bag. Whether she made it in five minutes or not she wasn't sure. The front door was open and Cornell was standing by it. She walked out, looking for the cab. She wasn't weeping but tears trickled steadily down her face and she scrubbed them away.

'I meant what I said, Simon. Someone is trying to get to you. I don't know who yet, but I will find out, and I will stop them.'

Cornell closed the door. Sam wanted to ask about the car, to scream that he couldn't leave her outside like this. It was cold, with the chill that exists only in the predawn of an early spring day, and she started to shiver. Sam walked towards the gate, then stopped to dig her phone out of her bag. Maybe she should call for her own cab, if she could get one at this time of night. She had just switched the phone on when she saw headlights coming down the road towards the house. A moment later a cab pulled up, and she climbed gratefully into the back seat.

'Where too, luv?' The cabbie was anonymous. His accent could have been from anywhere in the south-east, and in the light of the dashboard Sam could make out only that his skin was not Caucasian. She gave him her address.

'Sorry to dig you out of the office so late,' she added.

The cabbie laughed. 'Don't worry about it, luv. Rather be out on a nice long run like this than watching night-time telly.'

'We'd better stop at a cash point.'

'No need. This one's on the account.' He chuckled again. 'We get one of these most weekends, although not usually as late as this.'

Sam sat back in her seat, the cabbie's words were like a slap across her face, reminding her of what she was.

Sam let herself into her flat and threw her bag through the open door of the bedroom as she passed by on her way to the kitchen. She looked at the kettle but decided she needed something stronger than caffeine. There was a bottle of vodka in the fridge, and she poured herself a generous shot before dropping onto a chair at the tiny dining table.

What in heaven's name had she done? For the first time in more years than she could remember she had met someone who really meant something to her. She wasn't in love with him, not yet at least, but she felt drawn to him in so many other ways. They had been at the start of something, an adventure, and she had thrown it all away for the sake of her professional curiosity. How stupid could one person be?

She shifted position and the rubber she was still wearing squeaked softly. She had been aware of it throughout the taxi drive, horribly embarrassed in case the driver heard it, or smelt it, and she had vowed to rip it off as soon as she got home. The driver had said nothing, though, and now she didn't want to take it off. It was her last link to Simon, and felt warm, comforting. She had kicked off her trainers and could see the pink booties with their little frill. She pointed her toes.

The vodka was not helping. It had burned all the way down, but was settled uncomfortably in her stomach and gnawing at her like acid. She ran her hand through her hair, grabbing at it and pulling as if in penance for the terrible thing she had done to them both. Finally, the tears she had been refusing to give way to, ever since she had been told to leave Simon's house, broke through and she began to weep.

When Sam woke on Monday morning she decided she felt like shit. Sunday had also gone pear-shaped on her, and was the sort of day she was going to do her best to forget as quickly as possible. She had managed to take off the rubber play-set, and had even washed it before taking a bath, but had then found herself looking at it and fighting the urge to put it back on. Sunday breakfast had been delayed due to an absence of drinkable milk, and the trip to the supermarket had not only remedied that but had also sourced a bag of the strongest filter coffee she could find, whiskey to replace the inadequate vodka, a rare packet of cigarettes and several packets of appallingly calorific biscuits.

The filter machine had not been switched off all

day, and the cigarettes had been gone by lunchtime. By mid-afternoon her throat had been scorched, her chest felt tight, and her hands shook.

At least once an hour she had tried Hanshaw's mobile or started dialling Simon's number. Hanshaw had never picked up, and she had never finished calling Simon. Simon had already rejected her, with good reason, and if he had picked up, what could she have said that wouldn't have resulted in him rejecting her all over again?

At some point in the evening she had fallen asleep on the sofa.

Now it was Monday morning, she was awake again, but still curled in a ball on the sofa. Her back screamed in painful protest as she sat up, then she was wracked by a hacking cough. The urge for a smoke spiked in her throat.

For a moment she considered switching off her phone and excluding the world for another day, but Hanshaw would be furious if she didn't report. She dragged herself under the shower and switched it to a stinging, pulsing spray.

As she let the water pound into her shoulders, Sam felt a change wash over her. Her back straightened, her head lifted and she felt muscles bunch as they drew her jaw tight. The best idea she had been able to come up with the day before had been that she would resign, today and in person. The thought had cheered her up even more when she had realised it would give her the opportunity to deliver a few personal opinions too. Then, she would just have to forget about Simon Cornell and focus on her other clients.

Now, as the water sluiced away the despondency of the weekend, a better option occurred to her. She would prove Simon innocent. Prove to him and anybody else who was interested that there was nothing to the allegations against him, and prove to him that she had never been out to hurt him. *Then* she would tell him to bugger off and focus on her other clients. A large dose of *I told you so* would be ideal for her ego right now.

She laid out her best dark power suit, but couldn't help feeling a twinge of regret as she pulled on bra, panties and tights. They all seemed so conventional, so boring. She ripped them all off and tried again, hunting through her wardrobe for the sexiest underwear she could find. She found a black Basque she had forgotten she owned, a pair of seamed black stockings and a pair of court shoes with oversize heels. It was still like methadone to an H user, but she needed something to make her feel just a part of the woman Cornell had shown to her. She hunted for a pair of panties to match the spirit of the outfit and, when she found none, decided that was an omen and simply put on her suit.

Sam walked through the door at the agency and was greeted by the expectant expressions of Tony and Joy. Both faces fell as soon as they recognised her.

'Warm welcome,' said Sam caustically

'We wondered if you were the boss,' Tony explained.

Sam looked at her watch; half past ten. 'Hanshaw's not here?'

Joy shook her head. 'No, and there's no message to say he was going to be late.'

Sam frowned. Hanshaw was anal about punctuality – his own and others'. It didn't mean he was always where he said he was going to be, but he always kept in touch. 'Have you tried him at home?'

'He's not answering his mobile,' said Tony. 'Straight to voicemail. No sign of life at his place though. Not on Saturday, anyway.'

'You've tried the home number?'

'No answer,' said Joy, 'but then I can't remember the last time I called him on that number. It might not be working.'

'I couldn't get him over the weekend either. Is he working on anything dodgy at the moment?'

'Just this Cornell number,' said Joy, then her face paled. 'Oh damn! She'll be here at 11.'

'Who?'

'The snooty little cow who comes in for the progress reports,' said Tony. 'Every Monday at 11. Acts like her shit doesn't stink, and Mr Hanshaw fawns over her like she's royalty.'

Sam tried not to let her voice or expression change, but inside her fury started to burn. This must be the contact for whoever was trying to get at Simon.

'Leave her to me.'

14

'Are you sure?' asked Joy. 'Wouldn't it be better just to stall her? Say Mr Hanshaw's got a tummy bug or something?'

'I don't think so. Something's going on here, and I think this person might be able to give us some answers. Besides, I've got a feeling that Hanshaw's disappearance is something to do with this job.'

'Could be,' said Tony. 'He got me to follow her last week.'

'Did he say why?'

'No, but I don't think he liked what I found out. Seems this woman works for the target.'

'What?'

'Oh, and she's up to something really weird at some old pile in Botany Bay. Caught her answering the door in some crazy maid outfit.'

'Oh I *definitely* want a word with this girl,' Sam could feel her lips pressed angrily together.

'Please don't do anything rash, Miss Taylor,' said Joy. 'I don't think Mr Hanshaw would be very happy if you lost him this case.'

'Joy, I have a feeling that if I don't get some

answers from this woman then Mr Hanshaw might not be in any condition to worry about anything.'

'You think something's happened to him?'

'Perhaps. Let's start by getting some answers rather than making guesses.'

Sam strode through into Hanshaw's office and made herself comfortable at his desk. Tony leaned against a wall by the door while they waited for the messenger to arrive. The smell of cigars still clinging to the room wasn't an unpleasant one, not like cigarettes, and there was a sweet tang underneath, like sherry.

Sam fidgeted in the chair, surprised that Hanshaw would put up with something so uncomfortable – until she realised that the leather of the seat was moulded to the backside of its owner. She was just an interloper, a squatter, and the chair saw no reason to make her comfortable.

They heard the door of the outer office open at exactly 11. Sam straightened in the chair and Tony levered himself off the wall. There was a murmur of conversation then the door to the office opened and a woman stepped in. She had taken several steps into the room before she realised it was not Hanshaw at the desk. Her head came up like a startled deer's and she froze. Sam caught Tony's eye and flicked her gaze at the door. As if rehearsed, Tony pushed the door shut and leant against it. The expression on the woman's face turned from surprise to concern.

'What is the meaning of this? Where is Mr Hanshaw?'

'Sit down, please,' said Sam, waving at the chair opposite her but not making eye contact. She lowered her head so it looked like she was studying something on the desk, but she was watching the woman through her eyelashes.

'I asked you where Mr Hanshaw was,' the woman repeated. She didn't move any closer to the chair, and her voice had risen a fifth of an octave.

Sam raised her head and slowly looked the visitor over; not insultingly but in detail enough to make it clear that she wasn't intimidated. Also, the term 'woman' wasn't entirely appropriate. Although her clothing was stiff and formal, and was matched by heavy make-up, Sam realised that the visitor was little more than a girl.

'Let's keep this polite, miss. I'd really like you to sit down. Now.'

There was a tinge of fear on the girl's face now. She looked over her shoulder at an impassive Tony, then nervously walked across to the desk and lowered herself into the chair. Sam worked hard not to raise an eyebrow. The girl was wearing snug leather gloves and ankle boots; very Victorian, very chic, and with extraordinary heels. What was odd was that she could walk reasonably well in them. It made her gait unusual, but not inelegant. Sam doubted she would be so poised.

The other thing that niggled at her was the girl seemed too stiff, as though she might have a bad back. She sat rigidly in the seat. There was something else, too, but Sam had missed it. She scratched at her brain for a moment to see if she could jar it loose, but there wasn't time.

'Mr Hanshaw is not available. Perhaps I can assist you?'

'I doubt it, unless you can deliver the progress report I am to collect for my client.'

The girl had been going to use a different word. Her lips had taken on, just for an instant, the wrong shape for a 'cl'. The more time Sam spent with the girl, the more she felt there was something unexplained, something false. The attitude was an act, a veneer so thin that Sam could have poked through it in an instant. It was almost as though the girl was following a script she had been given. Now she was being forced to ad-lib, and she was creaking under the strain.

'I am fully aware of all Mr Hanshaw's current cases. It's you I am not aware of. If you'll give me your name, and tell me the nature of your business with Mr Hanshaw, I'm sure I shall be able to give you the report.'

She watched as the girl's façade crumbled a little further. The haughty manner disappeared entirely and she cast her eyes from side to side, as well as looking over her shoulder again at the door, and Tony leaning against it. 'I really should wait until I can see Mr Hanshaw. Is he expected any time soon?'

'No.'

'Perhaps I should return tomorrow.'

'Perhaps you should just tell me your name and what your business is here.'

'I can't,' the girl rose from her chair, afraid.

'I'm trying to be reasonable here.' Sam allowed a little of her anger to seep into her voice. The girl turned back to Sam and stared as if mesmerised by the authoritative tone. Sam watched as she pulled herself together and summoned her courage to make one last attempt to bully her way out of the situation. She almost felt sorry for her. She had thought the girl was about her age, but now she wondered if she was even out of her teens.

'I represent an important and wealthy client who will not be impressed by the way I've been treated, and I am sure that Mr Hanshaw will be more than disappointed if he loses this contract as a result of your actions. Now, if you allow me to leave this instant I shall say no more of this matter to my client.'

'Sit down,' Sam said, quietly.

'Weren't you listening? I said –'

'I heard you,' Sam snapped. 'Now you can sit down and listen to me, or I can ask my colleague there to help you sit down.'

Picking up on his cue Tony pushed himself away from the door with his elbows and took two steps towards the chair. The girl quickly sat again, but this time Sam spotted what it was she had missed. As the girl settled on the seat, she *winced.* A little flicker of discomfort, mixed with something else, rippled across the girl's face for just an instant.

'Now,' said Sam. 'Why don't I tell you what I already know and then you can co-operate by filling in the blanks?'

'I won't tell you anything.'

'We'll see.' Sam slouched back in Hanshaw's chair and smiled at the girl in what she hoped was a predatory way. She wanted to look like a cat staring at a mouse. 'Shall I begin by telling you which case you are interested in?'

The girl feigned indifference.

'You are here regarding the Cornell case.'

'Who?'

'Do I really look that stupid? You, or someone you represent, contacted Hanshaw to gather enough dirt to do a character assassination on Simon Cornell.' Sam cut herself off, biting back the angry remarks she had been about to make about incriminating an innocent man. Perhaps she could use the point later, but now was not the time. Besides, the girl had, just for a moment, looked anguished at the accusation.

'I think you've got me confused with somebody else.' Her voice was quiet now, all trace of haughtiness gone and a slight accent starting to creep in. She stared at the top of the desk.

'I don't think so. Hanshaw described you fairly accurately. Besides which, my silent friend over there knows you by sight. In fact he knows all sorts of interesting things about you; where you live, where you work.'

'This isn't fair!'

Sam could see fear in the girl's eyes, and could hear the desperation she was trying to cover with one last burst of anger. 'No, missy. What isn't fair is that you work for the man you are so eager to frame.'

The girl gasped. Her skin went an unhealthy white and for a moment Sam worried she was going to faint. 'How do you know?' she whispered, her hands gripping at the edge of the desk. For the first time Sam noticed how thin the leather was, and how tight, and for a moment she flashed back to Saturday night. The thing that had bugged her earlier hovered around her head again, tantalising, out of reach like an orbiting fly.

'As I said, we had you followed. Now, as I see it there are three options here. We can phone Mr Cornell and see if he wants to bring in the police, or we can just bring in the police ourselves.'

'No.' The girl was a little too quick and a little too loud.

'Then I take it you are going to take the third option: to co-operate with me?'

'I can't,' the girl moaned, wringing her hands. 'I really can't.'

'Why not?'

Tears welled on her bottom lids, ready to stain her

cheeks with cheap mascara. 'Please, let me go.'

Sam chuckled. 'I don't think we would achieve much by that. I want answers out of you.'

'I can't.' This time a whisper.

'Then you leave me no options. Give me your bag.'

'No!'

'Give me your bag or I will have my associate hold you in the chair and I will take it from you. And if you think screaming would do any good, this is a very old building with very thick walls. Besides, you have this one chance to co-operate, right now, or I simply call the police. You can explain to them if you like.' She gave the girl a very direct 'I know your secrets' look, and prayed the messenger didn't call her bluff. Something was starting to make sense to her, but she was having trouble believing it.

The girl put her bag on the table, her face turning from ashen grey to flaming red as she did so. Sam hesitated for a moment, surprised by the girl's deep blush. She looked up at Tony. 'Would you wait outside, please?'

The odd-job man gave Sam a questioning look, then nodded and left the room. The girl's tension lessened a little, but she was still a rubber band ready to snap. Sam picked up the bag. It was on the expensive end of ordinary, not too big and not too small. It fitted the role and looked barely used. Sam was sure she heard something metallic clink within. She undid the clasp and upended it onto Hanshaw's desk.

Sam was proud of herself. She kept her face poker straight and ignored all the unconventional and interesting things that rolled over the desk. Instead she picked up only the thick brown envelope.

'I assume this is Mr Hanshaw's fee?' Sam tapped

the envelope on the desk. The girl nodded, apparently unable to take her eyes from a spot on the wall some two feet above Sam's head. The tears were trickling down her face now, leaving dark runnels. Sam debated allowing the girl a moment with a tissue. *Sod her*, she thought. *If it makes her feel uncomfortable it just makes the job easier for me.* She made no attempt to open the envelope, though her fingers ached to see how much Hanshaw was being paid, and she slipped it into a drawer of his desk. 'I'll make sure he gets this, and you can see Joy on your way out for a receipt. Now, let's see what else we can find out about you.'

A small purse had landed next to the envelope. Sam picked it up, opened it and tried to empty it on a different part of the desk. Nothing fell out. All that was inside was a driver's licence and a debit card, neatly tucked into little slots. No cash, no store cards or loyalty cards. Sam pulled out the driver's licence, drew over a pad of paper, and took several notes before she looked up.

'Karen Malden. Twenty years old and currently registered to an address in Reading.' Sam paused. 'Rather a long drive, isn't it? Reading must be a good 60 or 70 miles away, and on slow motorways.' The girl still said nothing, still stared at the wall. Sam sighed. 'Miss Malden, you really are making me do this the hard way. I *will* get what I want. It would be so much more helpful if you would just tell me? No? Very well. What is this Reading address? You know it's illegal not to keep the address on your driving license current?'

Karen fidgeted slightly, but kept her silence.

'Why don't you have it registered to your real address at Botany Bay?'

Karen let out a choked gasp and stared wildly into

Sam's face.

'Oh yes, we know far more about you than you think. Almost everything we need to know. Are you sure you don't want to co-operate?'

'Please, *please*, let me go. I want to, but I mustn't. I can't.'

Sam stirred the other items on the desk around; a pair of handcuffs with no key, a red ball gag large enough that Sam would not want to try it, a pair of clamps linked by a chain, and a micro-vibrator. She had a fairly good idea as to how the conversation ought to go, and even a notion as to how she might be able to turn the unexpected stash to her advantage. She sat back in the chair again and softened her voice.

'Do you know what I think, Karen? I think you are a pawn. I think you are doing this to shield somebody, and that this somebody has a hold on you. Is it love or fear, Karen? Or is it both?' Sam knew she had hit the mark when Karen flinched and looked guilty. 'Who do you serve, Karen? Is it him?' Sam was unprepared for the stab of pain and jealousy that ripped into her heart, and equally surprised when Karen shook her head miserably. Sam quickly changed track.

'Come on, Karen, these are not the sort of things you would carry about with you unless you were in service to someone, and you don't look like the sort who would be dominating ...' Sam's voice tailed off as an alternative struck her.

'A mistress. You serve a mistress.'

15

Karen was motionless for almost a minute, more tears coursing down her cheeks, before she finally nodded. Sam took pity on the girl and passed her a box of tissues. She finally had the leverage she had been searching for. She felt so smug that she put her feet up on the edge of Hanshaw's desk, and hid a smile as Karen's eyes grew round when she saw the shoes and stockings she was wearing. 'A little slut slave being put right in the middle of the firing line by some cowardly bitch of a mistress.'

Anger flickered in Karen's eyes. 'My mistress is not a coward.'

'Your mistress is a stinking coward,' Sam said more loudly, trying to inject some of the commanding tone Cornell had used so effectively on her. 'What else do you call someone who sends a child out to front for her? She's afraid, and she's abusing your loyalty by commanding you to go out and do her dirty work for her.'

'Don't talk about my mistress like that!' Karen shouted back.

Sam rose to her feet. 'You will not address me in that manner.' Her voice was icy. 'If you show such disrespect to one of your betters again I shall have you gagged until you remember your manners.'

From the look on Karen's face Sam guessed she was pitching it just right. Karen seemed to be reacting automatically to Sam's confident superiority, and Sam realised the weapon was far more potent than she had first thought. She decided to take a risk. Either it would further her position with the girl, or it would blow up catastrophically. She grinned inwardly. Risks were always fun.

'You seem to have forgotten your place, Karen. Do you normally treat your betters this way?'

'No,' Karen mumbled.

'No *what*?' hissed Sam.

The girl looked startled again, and a little confused. 'No, miss … mistress?'

'That's better. Come here and stand in front of me.' Sam waited until the girl had walked around to the side of the desk. 'Now put those cuffs on. Perhaps they will remind you to keep your place.'

'But there's no key.'

Sam slammed her hand on the table and made the girl jump. 'Did I ask you if there was? Put them on. Or shall I ask my colleague to help you?'

Panic flickered across Karen's face, quickly replaced by a sulky reluctance as she reached out for the cuffs. Sam felt excitement growing inside her as she watched the girl close the first bracelet, but she stopped her when she started on the second.

'Not in front of you. Behind.'

Karen gave her a pleading look, but Sam kept her own face resolute. With a tiny sigh, Karen put her hands behind her back and closed the second cuff with practised ease. Sam got out of the chair and stood as tall as she could, trying to loom over the younger girl.

'That's better, but I want you to look at me.' When Karen made no move to lift her eyes from the floor, Sam placed a finger under her chin and forced her head up. Their eyes locked and Sam refused to let her look away. She had got Karen almost where she wanted her now, and she gently stroked her thumb across the girl's bottom lip. Karen's mouth opened slightly, and Sam had to fight to stop herself slipping her thumb into the little slave's mouth and making her suck on it. 'How long have you been in service, slave?'

'A little over two years, mistress.'

'And have you always served the same owner?'

'Yes, mistress.'

'Then you have no experience of serving anybody else? A master?'

'My mistress has loaned me out to others, but I belong only to her.'

Sam still had her finger under Karen's chin, and their eyes were still locked, and for the first time she saw doubt in the girl's eyes. 'Slave, have you ever thought about what your responsibilities are to your mistress?'

'To serve her. To obey her.'

'Very proper. Now, what about her responsibilities to you?'

'To me? None. I gave myself to her.'

Sam took her fingers from under Karen's chin and brushed the back of her hand softly down the girl's cheek. She was almost sure she felt Karen lean in to the caress. 'You're wrong, Karen. The person to whom you have given yourself has greater responsibilities to you than you have to her.' Sam felt her eyes start to mist over. Responsibilities like not making you depend on them, then taking that support away. 'You have placed yourself entirely at her mercy, and given her free license to do what she will with you. In return, you have a right to expect your mistress to protect you.'

Sam's hand wandered slowly from Karen's cheek, down her neck, and to the buttons of her jacket. She undid them slowly and pulled the jacket down over Karen's shoulders. The blouse beneath was almost transparent, and Sam could see small, firm breasts with prominent nipples pushing against the tight fabric. 'A mistress should nurture her slave. Unless both parties are satisfied, there can be no happiness. Without happiness there is no relationship. Both parties must satisfy the needs of the other. Wouldn't you agree, Karen?'

She let the backs of her fingers stroke softly across Karen's nipples and the girl groaned. 'Please. What if someone comes in?'

Sam paused for a moment, then pinched Karen's nipples hard enough to make her wince. 'You may be right, but are presumptuous for saying so.' She leaned back across Hanshaw's desk and hit a button on the intercom. 'Joy? Nobody is to come in here until I say so. Not you, not Tony, not even Hanshaw himself. Clear?'

'Perfectly.'

Sam released the button and turned back to Karen. The moment had been broken by the distraction, but Sam figured it was probably for the best. Her own nipples were tingling, and her pussy felt hot. She was getting caught up in the moment again, not focusing on the job.

'Do you agree with me, Karen?'

The girl nodded mutely, embarrassed but aroused. Sam reached forward and started unbuttoning Karen's blouse. 'So doesn't that imply that your mistress is abusing you by making you put yourself in danger like this?'

'It's not like that.' Karen's voice was a breathy whisper as Sam undid the bottom button of the blouse. She pulled the blouse open and hid a grin. Karen was wearing a corset, heavily boned and laced punishingly tight. Sam felt a pang of jealousy. She ran her hands down it, from just under Karen's breasts to the snug narrowness of her waist, delighting in the feel of repressed tension, of control.

For a moment, she felt bad about what she was doing. She was taking something away from this girl. Something she herself had just lost, through her own stupidity; something that was still an aching absence. Was she doing this to punish someone, because she was lashing out? No, she was doing it for *her* master, to save him even, if he didn't want her any more. It sickened her that she would do to another what he had done to her, but if it meant protecting him, she would try. A bubble of bile burst in the back of her throat at the hypocrisy of her speech about responsibilities.

Sam reached forwards and took Karen's nipples between thumb and finger, rolling them gently. 'I can satisfy your needs, Karen. I can give you everything you want.'

'Please stop,' Karen breathed, but her back was arched and her mouth hung open.

'You dare tell me what to do?' said Sam, releasing Karen's breasts and reaching for the nipple clamps on the desk. She wished she had had more time to study them. They were far more delicate than the ones Simon had used on her, and looked as though you could wear them under almost anything and they wouldn't be seen. Karen had taken a half-step back, but Sam hooked a finger into the top of the corset and pulled her back.

'Stay still, or would you like me to ask Tony to put them on for you?' It took just a moment to figure how the clamps worked, then she gently closed the first around Karen's left nipple. It fastened with a soft *snick* and Karen gasped, the cuffs rattling as she instinctively tried to free her hands. Sam gave her no time to think or adjust and slipped the second clamp into place.

Karen moaned softly and rolled her shoulders forwards in an ecstatic motion. Sam thought she looked beautiful; bound, clamped, controlled. She reached forwards and twisted her fingers into the hair at the back of Karen's head, pulling the girl's face back to meet hers. Karen's eyes were filmed with lust, and her lips were already parted. Sam possessed her mouth, forcing her tongue between Karen's teeth, demanding her surrender. Karen stiffened, resisted, just for a moment, then relaxed against Sam, giving herself. Sam reached down and put her hand under Karen's skirt, intending to toy with her sex. All she felt was warm metal. A chastity belt? The thought inflamed her further. Denied the girl's sex, Sam hooked a finger into the nipple chain. Little tugs and twists soon had Karen whimpering into Sam's mouth.

Eventually Sam pulled away, just far enough to move her mouth to Karen's ear. 'Tell me,' she whispered. For a heartbeat, she thought she might have broken the girl, then came a slow shake of the head. Sam moved back until she could see Karen's face. She looked stricken, lost, and still lustful.

'I can't.'

Sam would not meet Karen's eyes again, and said nothing as she buttoned first the blouse, then the jacket. The rest of Karen's things were stuffed into her bag. She could hear Karen sniffling, presumably crying, but still couldn't look. She was fighting off the fantasy of holding Karen's face against her sex as the girl made her come. This wasn't going to work.

'What about the clamps,' Karen asked.

'You've disappointed me,' Sam answered. 'I believe a little punishment is due.' She reached across the desk and pushed the intercom button. 'Tony? Get in here.'

The door was opening before she had taken her finger from the button, and Tony's face suggested he was expecting trouble.

'Miss Marden is still reluctant to assist us. Unfortunately she appears to have become entangled in a set of cuffs for which she has no key.'

'Oh dear, how sad,' said Tony, grinning.

'The address on Miss Marden's driver's licence is in Reading, but she seems unwilling, or unable, to supply us with any closer address where we might be able to find some help for her. Can you think of anywhere else we could try?'

Tony put on a comic thinking face. 'It's a long shot, but for some reason I think we might be able to get something out of a place called The Manse, in Botany Bay.'

Karen looked devastated as Tony trotted out the address.

'You see, Karen,' Sam said, not unsympathetically. 'We know much more about you than you think we do. Are you sure you don't want to reconsider?'

Karen shook her head, miserably. Sam dug through the girl's bag until she found a set of house keys. 'Tony, keep an eye on her. She's not to leave until I get back.'

'Yes, boss.'

Sam flashed him a grin at the title, not sure if it was for the girl's benefit or if he meant it. She stood up. 'I think I fancy a quick trip to the colonies.'

A phone rang. It wasn't Sam's ring tone, and when she looked to Tony he shook his head and shrugged. Karen was blushing furiously. Sam patted the pockets of the girl's jacket and found a tiny Nokia. The display said 'Unknown Number'. Sam put the phone on the desk, careful not to answer it, then looked at Tony and shook her head.

He nodded once to say he got that nobody was to touch the phone. 'Her boss?'

'Almost certainly. Checking up to see why she's late.'

The phone stopped ringing. 'Well, he knows something's wrong now.'

'Yes, but not what. Let's keep it that way.'

'Want me to get her to make up some excuse if it rings again?'

Sam shook her head. 'She may have code words we don't know anything about. Let's just leave whoever is on the other end of the phone guessing.'

Tony nodded, and Sam headed out through the door.

Tony steered the girl to a chair and sat her down, then perched himself on the edge of Hanshaw's desk. She was pretty sweet if you looked past the overdone make-up. Nice eyes. He offered he one of his best smiles. 'You need anything? Water, maybe?'

She gave him a shy smile. 'A key would be nice.' She rattled the cuffs. 'Don't suppose you have one lying around?'

'I could probably sort something out. Only one problem.'

'What?'

'Boss said I couldn't.' He grinned at her. 'Sorry.'

The shy smile became a little plastic for a moment, but didn't slip too far. 'Can't think why. I'm nothing. Nobody important.' Tony shook his head but said nothing. The smile shifted from nice to naughty. 'I can make it worth it.'

Tony decided to play along. It was a way to pass the time if nothing else. 'Yeah? Doesn't look to me like you've got much to trade.'

'I could have if you helped me take these off.'

Tony shook his head again but the girl didn't seem inclined to take no for an answer. She rose from the chair and stepped towards him. Tony pushed himself away from the desk. He wasn't sure what she was up to, but he wanted to be ready in case she tried to run for it. Instead, she stepped even closer and turned her back to him.

She was too close, and Tony took a step back. When she kept crowding him he took another – and found himself pinned against the desk. The girl – Karen? – looked over her shoulder and actually batted her eyelashes at him. He'd never seen anybody do it before. 'My, I do believe he's shy.'

Her hands cupped together over his prick. Tony pushed them away, but couldn't stop his cock registering its approval. Karen looked over her shoulder at him again. 'I entertain you, you let me out go?'

Tony briefly considered the morality of the situation, and while he mused, Karen stroked her fingers up and down the fly of his trousers. Tony's prick decided the situation for him. She was still looking over her shoulder, so he smiled and shrugged. He had no intention of helping. All right, it was still a lie, but he could knew he could get away with it. He also wanted to see how she would manage with the cuffs on.

She surprised him. While one hand gently stroked his glans through his jeans, the other was reaching for his belt buckle, then the button at his waist. It was as though this was something she had practiced. She dragged the zipper down on his fly, then took hold of his waistband and did a sort of shimmy as she squatted down to her heels, pulling his jeans down to his knees as she went.

The girl straightened up and he expected her to do the same thing with his briefs. She didn't. Her hands folded around his cock, this time with only the thin cotton of his underwear as a barrier, and she caressed him. In less than a minute he was fully erect, hard enough to ache. He was already having to take steps to stop himself from unloading into his pants, and was actually relieved when she took her hands off him and turned around.

'Are you ready?' she asked, running her tongue over her lips. 'Are you ready to fuck my face, all handcuffed and helpless?'

Karen sank to her knees. His briefs were still over his cock, tenting upwards. She kissed the bulge, then reached up and snagged the waistband with her teeth. Carefully, delicately, she pulled the elastic up, then out. Tony held his breath. If she messed this up, if the elastic snapped back on his cock, this little treat could end real fast. She gently eased the waistband down, releasing it carefully to snug up behind his scrotum.

A moist, warm tickle made him twitch as she licked his scrotum then kissed each of his balls. Tony wanted to grab her hair, pull her into position, and fuck her face – and yet somehow it didn't seem fair for him to use his hands when she couldn't. Her tongue touched the base of his shaft and glided upwards to the tip of his glans. Tony shuddered and thought of motorbike engines. When he looked down, his cock was resting on her tongue, her mouth open, teasing him. He eased forward and she pulled away. He tried again more quickly, and she pulled back further for a moment before bright red lips closed around his knob and slid hungrily down his shaft.

Tony had been on the receiving end of oral sex before, but this girl was so good it was shocking. He'd had no complaints, but Tony knew he was no horse. Still, it was unusual to feel a nose touch his pelvis at the same time as his cock touched the back of a woman's throat. And Karen looked like she could stay there all day. She was even looking up at him, watching him.

Her lips slid back up his shaft, holding him firmly, sucking gently, until just his glans was still in her mouth. Her tongue darted around it, tickling his piss-hole and at the sensitive spot on the underside of the bell. Tony shuddered again and gripped the edge of Hanshaw's desk. As if she knew she had him, the girl started to slide up and down his prick. Tony could take it for only a few moments. He cried out as he shot his first load into her mouth, then – with her head bobbing down for each fresh spurt – grunted until he was done.

Tony's legs felt weak, and at some point he had screwed his eyes shut. When he opened them and looked down, the girl slowly drew her lips off the end of his cock, then poked her cupped tongue out. His jism puddled on her tongue. She slowly drew the tongue back in, swallowed very obviously, then poked it out again to show it was clean. Tony rubbed his left hand through his hair for a moment, then pulled up his briefs and his trousers before putting his hands under Karen's arms and helping her to her feet.

'Good?' she asked.

'Un-fucking-believable,' Tony replied, knowing his grin was inane but not being able to do anything about it.

'Wonderful. Now get these cuffs off me.'

'Sorry.'

The girl moved in slow motion as her head came up to bore gimlet eyes into Tony's face. 'You promised.'

'And I will let you out of those cuffs. Just as soon as we can get hold of a key. Which will be some time after Miss Taylor gets back.'

Karen dropped onto a chair. 'Bastard.'

Tony's grin just kept getting wider.

Sam fumed. The traffic had been unusually awful and it had taken her much longer to get to Botany Bay than she had expected. Arriving at one o'clock did not give her as much time as she had hoped to snoop around. Rather than pulling into the drive, she parked in the closest side road. She didn't want her car to be blocked in if anybody arrived at the house while she was inside. Less chance they could stop her if she was on foot. On the downside, the side road was a good hundred yards away from the drive.

The best cover was to look like you had nothing to hide. She would walk boldly up to the front door and ring the doorbell. If anybody answered, she could ask for someone she knew wasn't there and claim she had got the address wrong. She rang the bell and knocked loudly, then peered through a couple of windows at the front. Anybody inside would have seen her as a persistent sales caller and sent her away, so Sam was fairly confident there was nobody in the house.

She took a small black box from her pocket – a gift from a friend with a slightly dubious past – and ran it around the door frame. The box searched for wires or magnets, but no lights flashed and no speaker beeped. There could still be a motion detector covering the hall, but she would only know that when she opened the door.

There were only two keys on the ring she had taken from Karen, but before she retrieved them from her pocket she slipped on a pair of purple surgical gloves. No point leaving her prints all over the place. The heavy five-lever Chubb obviously fitted the mortise lock, and the thinner key turned easily in the cylinder. A moment later she was inside and the door was closed behind her. A quick sweep around the walls showed no other detectors, and there was no keypad near the door. The house was, surprisingly, unprotected.

Sam snubbed the catch on the cylinder, locking it, then put the Chubb key back in the mortise and turned it half way around. Now nobody could get in through that door, and she had a good chance of a warning if someone disturbed her. Sam began to explore.

Covert house searches were not something she did every day, but she did enough of them to have developed a routine to cover the most space in the least time. She usually took a quick look into every room first, floor by floor, to get a feel for the most interesting places. Starting at the top and working down was another habit.

She trotted up the stairs and started opening doors; one bathroom, one toilet, one master bedroom with an *en-suite* and two guest bedrooms, also with *en-suite*. She paused at the master bedroom, guessing this was where Karen's mistress slept, and gave it a more careful examination.

There was nothing of interest, either related to the case or otherwise. Sam went around twice, not believing the room could be so sterile. It was just a bedroom with ordinary – if expensive – clothes and mundane jewellery. There were no personal touches; no photos, no sentimental ornaments. It felt like a hotel room.

There was only one door left to check on that floor and Sam knew instantly that she had found Karen's room. The décor was dark and severe. Black curtains covered a tiny window, and although there was an *en-suite*, it was white and stark and medical in its austerity. All around the bedroom there were metal rings fixed to pieces of furniture and bolted to the walls and ceiling, with no attempt made to disguise them. Sam touched one of the heavy brackets screwed into the bottom of the bed and shivered.

Wardrobes were built into one wall, and there was a dressing table with a mirror opposite them. Sam opened one of the wardrobe doors and looked inside. There was a small collection of conventional clothing, but the majority of the space was taken up by 'specialist' attire. Sam ran her hand along some hanging items, and found herself aroused and repelled at the same time.

She tore herself away. Fascinating though it was to see where she might have travelled with Simon, that wasn't what she was here for, and she was wasting time. She went downstairs and scanned through the rooms. Most she discounted after only a quick glance. Dining room, kitchen and lounge were not going to help her. They were as austere and untouched as the master bedroom. Another odd thought began to poke at her: the place looked like a film set or a show home than a place people actually lived. Everything was too well co-ordinated, like someone had been told to fill an otherwise empty house.

The study seemed like the best, perhaps only, place for a detailed search, and Sam was about to embark on this when she realised there was still one other door she hadn't yet opened, at the end of the hall. From the layout of the house, she guessed it could lead only a store room or a box room, but it was still worth checking out.

The door didn't lead to a room. Behind it was a flight of stairs. She found the light switch, and the harsh glare of a bare bulb revealed another door at the bottom. In Sam's experience, cellars were dark and dingy places full of either junk or wine, and she almost turned away. Suddenly however something on the lower door caught her eye. She looked more carefully, and saw there it was a bolt. Why would anybody put a bolt on the outside of a cellar door?

As Sam walked down the stairs the hairs on her arms stood up. She paused half way down, the sensation spooking her. Had she heard something? She brushed the feeling aside, blaming it on the cooler air below the house.

There were two light switches next to the lower door. She flicked one and plunged herself into darkness. Cursing the stab of fear that made her heart hammer in her chest, she returned that switch to its original position, restoring the light in the stairwell, and then flicked the other. Nothing happened. She pulled back the bolt and pushed the door open.

Sam was quite pleased with herself that all she did was purse her lips and raise her eyebrows. It wasn't ever day she walked into a fully equipped dungeon. The room was cold, physically and emotionally. The décor was clinical and the equipment utterly functional. There was an ominous grating in the middle of the room that looked like a shower drain.

The room repulsed her, radiating a feeling of negativity that made her heart feel heavy just standing on the threshold. She flicked off the room light and closed and bolted the door before pattering quickly back up the stairs. She still had work to do.

The study was still the only promising room. All the others had a sterile feel to them, strictly conforming to their function and nothing else. Either Karen's mistress had OCD or Karen was one hell of a housekeeper. If there was going to be anything, it would be in here.

A superficial examination of the furniture in the study was disappointing. It seemed that whoever had planned the room had gone out of their way to prove that it had nothing to hide. There were no cupboards or filing cabinets or elegant bookcases with glass-fronted doors; just open shelves and tables. The only thing with any drawers was the desk. It was a ponderous thing, bigger than Hanshaw's and made of either genuine- or faux-Regency mahogany. Sam sat in the desk chair and, after pushing away a melancholy sense of *déjà vu*, started going through the drawers.

Nothing was locked, and most of the drawers were empty. One held letter-writing paper and envelopes, another pens and pencils. Everything she touched seemed to reinforce the feeling she was in a hotel suite, and she fought the urge to slam the drawers shut in frustration. She couldn't believe that there was nothing. She had been in the house almost an hour and so far it looked like a total waste of time. There must be something she had missed.

She replayed her trip through the house. Perhaps she should go and check all the drawers in the kitchen? People sometimes kept stuff there. She ignored the impulse to move and carried on mentally retracing her steps. Suddenly she threw her hands up in disgust.

'Fuck. *Stupid* bitch.'

Sam was on her feet and heading for the basement stairs a second later. She ran down the stairs so fast that she nearly arrived at the lower door face first, and was throwing it open before she had switched the light on. Inside the dungeon, on the wall to the left, tucked between a rack of devices for doling out pain and a metal X-frame, was another small door. She tried the handle, fearing it would be locked, but it turned easily and the door swung open into a dark space filled with pinpoints of multicoloured light.

At first Sam thought it was a recording studio. One monitor showed a feed from Karen's room and another a view of the dungeon. She cursed. If either of those feeds was recording, then she would be identifiable. That could be a breaking-and-entering charge right there, unless she could somehow get Karen to crack and say she had given her permission. The rest of the stuff was computer equipment. Sam was savvy enough to recognise some networking kit and a rack full of powerful-looking servers. Was Karen's mistress streaming the poor girl's torments out to the net?

There was no documentation in the room, and Sam didn't really want to start messing with the computers, realising she didn't know enough about them. But she was sure the answers were in those servers somewhere. Her hands hovered briefly over the only keyboard she could see, temptation goading her to try something, anything, but she knew she was in over her head and needed help.

It still made no sense to her that all that equipment was there and yet the place had no security; not even a burglar alarm. She closed the door to the server room and walked across the dungeon to the stairs. As she switched the lights out, she wondered if they – whoever they were – thought they could rely on a 'purloined letter' trick. If there were no expensive security devices installed, who would ever know that the house was worthy of attention? They were hiding in plain sight.

She glanced at her watch and swore again. She had been in the house over an hour. Too long. She left the way she had come in, carefully relocking everything to minimise the risk that anyone would realise there had been an intruder and come looking for her. She peeled the surgical gloves off her hands as she walked down the drive and stuffed them back into her pocket.

Once back in the relative safety of her battered Polo, she had the luxury of time to think about what she had seen. Nothing made sense. There was not a single piece of paper in the house that bore the name of either the mistress or Karen. There was no way that could be an accident. Something was always left lying around – a bill, a letter. The only fact Sam had walked away with was that whoever this mistress was, she was taking absurd pains to hide her identity. She started the car and drove off. As she passed the drive of the house, her heart almost stopped. A top-of-the-range Audi and a battered Escort were now parked untidily in the drive. She took a firmer grip on the steering wheel and put her foot down. She had to get back to Hanshaw's office. There was a call she needed to make.

16

Diana Cartwright never panicked. Occasionally, she felt the urge to, but she never allowed it to actually happen. At this moment, she felt the urge. Something had gone wrong. She did not yet know what, or how badly. For the fifth time, she picked up the phone and dialled the number of her slave's mobile. She let it ring a dozen or so times, then hung up.

It would have been easy to give in to the impulse to be angry with Karen; it was, after all, almost certainly going to be her fault. The standard procedure, which had been drummed into the girl at the end of a riding crop, was that she should stop as soon as she was out of sight of that disgusting little detective's office and call in. Getting the progress report should have taken her no more than ten minutes, and the little fool should have called by 11.30 at the latest.

Now it was past one o'clock. It was possible that the explanation was totally innocent, but there was nothing that she could think of other than a serious road accident or sudden ill health. She allowed herself a savage grin. If either of those were the case, the little slut would have endless fun explaining her outfit to the hospital staff. The grin faded away. It was more likely that some other force had intervened. However unpalatable the thought, she had to consider the possibility that her security had been compromised.

Once she had made the decision to act, she felt more relaxed. If she was doing something, then she was in control. She closed her laptop and removed the security fob. The laptop went into its bag and the fob went into an inside pocket of her jacket. Then she paid a visit to Ryk Richards.

She usually had him report to her, preferably at her home, but on this occasion it did not seem appropriate. She entered his office without knocking and saw him hurriedly blank something from his computer screen at the same time as he twitched his right hand away from his crotch. She guessed he had been scanning through some of the less socially acceptable areas of the internet, or perhaps even the private little feed that she had given him access to. She wanted to be annoyed. She was paying him a generous stipend on top of his company salary and was not best pleased to find him wasting his time looking at porn. There were, however, more important things to worry about and she let the matter drop.

She drew breath to speak, but her hand lifted automatically to cover her nose as she inhaled the baleful odour of the place. She had expected that the tiny office would be stuffy, but the addition of stale sweat, pizza and something she recognised but did not want to think about caused a tiny bubble of bile to burst in her throat.

'Have you ever considered opening the window in here?' she asked.

Richards shrugged. 'The wind blows my paperwork around.'

Cartwright realised it was an argument she could not win and again let it pass. 'I think we have to move you away from here. When could be ready to relocate to the house?'

'Wednesday, maybe. Perhaps late on Tuesday if I cut some corners. Wassup?'

'I was thinking of minutes rather than days.'

The colour slowly drained from Richard's face and his hands began to shake. 'Something's gone wrong, hasn't it?' he moaned. 'Oh, God. I should have known this would happen. I knew this was too good to be true.'

'Nothing has gone wrong – at least nothing I can be sure of. I just want you to move to the house as a precaution.'

'Pretty drastic for a precaution.' Richards voice had risen, and his arms were waving about in agitation. 'Why the rush, eh? If it's just a precaution, why all the bloody hurry?'

'Keep your voice down,' she hissed. 'Do you want everybody in the building to hear your whining?'

'What happened? Who found out about us?'

She took a deep breath and tried to contain her anger. Killing him after he had completed his job for her began to seem like such a splendid idea. It would beat paying him the money she had promised. 'Will you stop acting like an idiot? All I know is that that worthless little slave of mine is overdue checking in and I cannot get an answer from her. As a precaution – and I repeat, precaution – I want you to move operations to the house. Do you understand now? Have I driven the point through your overly-dense skull?'

Richards did not appear to be listening to her. He was rocking from side to side, his hands tightly clenched between his knees and his chair creaking alarmingly.

Cartwright just managed to push down the urge to slap him across the back of his head, mainly by thinking how his matted, greasy hair would feel against her hand. She settled for grabbing the fabric of his T-shirt at the shoulder and using it to shake him.

'Snap out of it, you fool. Pull yourself together.'

'I knew this would happen. I knew this was going to get me in trouble. What if the police find out? They'll lock me up. I'll die in prison.'

'If you don't stop this whining I'll kill you myself,' she snapped, then grimaced when she realised her own voice had been too loud. Damn the man for getting under her skin.

Richards wasn't listening. He was wrapped up in his private world of self-pity. 'I've had enough. I want out. I don't want anything more to do with this.'

She opened the front flap of her laptop bag and took out a Walther P22 semi-automatic pistol. She put the case on the floor and eased the hammer back with a menacing triple click. The already-unpleasant odour in the room was joined by Richard's acrid fear-stench as he realised that what she was holding was not a toy.

'This may not look as intimidating as some of the more preposterous weapons you see on television,' said Cartwright coldly, 'but I am told that shooting someone in the head with it will kill them, and it makes no more noise than a door slamming. Now, unless you want to end your career permanently I suggest you stop your pathetic whining and do whatever you have to do before we depart. I will leave now. You will leave in ten minutes. I will be watching. If you don't appear I will call the police.'

Richards clicked his mouse twice and pulled a memory stick from the front of his PC. 'Done.'

'Did you delete all the evidence?' She frowned. His readiness to leave now seemed unreasonably quick.

'Everything is on the stick. Nothing is kept on the PC or on any company system.'

'Leave in ten minutes as planned, then meet me back at the house as soon as you can get there.'

She eased the hammer down on the Walther, slid the safety on, and put it back in her case. As she walked from the office, she tried not to make too obvious her relief to be stepping out into cleaner air. Her plans were too close to fruition to allow a minor complication to delay them. Once the payload was delivered, and a simple demonstration had proven it worked, the auction would be held. One bid for control of the current infestation in the London Equities market, the other for the raw technology. What the new owners did with the technology was up to them, but she was hoping to watch fires burn across Europe's stock markets.

Sam pulled up noisily outside Hanshaw's offices, abandoning the Polo at an untidy angle across two parking bays. She ran up the stairs two at a time, bursting dramatically into Joy's outer office. 'Any word from Hanshaw?'

Joy only had time to shake her head as Sam bustled though the inner door into Hanshaw's sanctum. She strode directly up to Karen, grabbed her by the lapels and hauled her out of the chair.

'She was recording you. Did you know that? One camera in your room, another in the basement.'

Karen's face went white and horror filled her eyes. 'No!'

'I saw the image feeds, and those were the only

two. I'd hazard a guess they were hooked up to the net, too. Do you think she sold you just to a select few, or were you the star of your own website?'

Sam felt the weight pull on the jacket as Karen's knees buckled beneath her. She guided the girl to a safe landing on the chair, then leaned against the desk. 'Karen, she was using you – had used you – in every wrong way she could. You must see that any loyalty you have is misplaced. Please, tell us what we need to know.'

There was a long pause, but Sam didn't push it. She could feel the girl was broken, that it was just a matter of time.

Eventually Karen spoke. 'There are two of them. A man. He works at SCCS too. His name is Ryk Richards. And my mistress is … was? … Diana Cartwright.'

'And what are they doing?'

'I don't know. Richards comes to the house to report on something, and all my m … all she ever asks is when it will be ready. They never say what it is.'

'And who is this Cartwright woman? What part does she play?'

'She works at SCCS too. She's Mr Cornell's business partner.'

Karen and Tony watched bewildered as Sam grabbed hold of the phone and started punching buttons. The ring tone in her ear was replaced by the cool voice of a receptionist. 'Simon Cornell, please,' she asked, fighting to keep her voice calm.

'Who should I say is calling?'

'Sam Taylor.'

A pause, then, 'I'm sorry, Mr Cornell is in a meeting and can't take your call.'

'I don't care if he is on the toilet, put me through.'

'I'm sorry. Can I take a message?'

'No you cannot take a bloody message,' Sam yelled. 'Wait, there *is* a message. You can tell him that if he is not on the other end of this line in 60 seconds then I go to the newspapers.'

There was another pause during which Sam could almost taste the curiosity radiating from the telephonist. There was a muted 'Please hold', then some cheap muzak. Almost double the allotted minute passed before Sam heard a click and the music was cut off.

'What the hell do you want?' his voice was music to her ears, but the bitterness was a knife to her heart.

'Simon. Thank God.'

'I doubt he has anything to do with you, and neither do I. I thought I made that perfectly clear. I am in the middle of an important meeting. If you have anything to say to me get on with it or hang up.'

'I need you to come to my boss's office. Right now.'

'Impossible.'

'Please, Simon. It's important.'

'To whom?'

'Both of us. Look, I know you don't think too much of me right now, but do you really think I would be doing this if I didn't have to?'

'I no longer have any idea what your motives might be.'

'For fuck's sake, Cornell. I'm trying to help you here. *Still* trying to help you. You are being set up and it looks like an inside job. I've almost got enough to stop whatever is going on, but I need your help. Now if you still want to play the injured party, that's fine and I'll let you go to whichever hell you choose.'

Cornell hesitated before he answered. 'I'll think about it.'

'Thanks very much.' Sam almost managed to keep

the sarcasm out of her voice, then she gave him the address. 'Don't think too long, mister. I'm holding a witness here, but if you aren't here in an hour, I'll let her go, wash my hands, and pretend this whole thing never happened.'

She put the phone down before he could say anything else. Karen and Tony were looking at her as though they wanted to edge away from her a little. She stared back at them for a moment, then covered her face with her hands. She felt wasted, physically and mentally. All she wanted was a long bath, a bottle of cold wine, and a pizza – possibly all together. None seemed likely for far too long.

'Take those cuffs off her, Tony. We wouldn't want Mr Cornell getting the wrong idea. Then take her down to the toilet. Don't let her out of your sight. If you let her get away, I'll rip your balls off.'

'Promises, promises, boss,' grinned Tony. He stole a paperclip from Hanshaw's desk, bent over the last quarter inch or so and picked the locks of the cuffs quicker than if he had held the key in his fingers. Karen swung her arms a few times and then, as she rubbed her wrists, delivered such a venomous glare at Tony that Sam almost laughed. Tony gave the girl a moment or two, then took her firmly by the upper arm and guided her towards the door.

'Bring some coffee back with you,' Sam called. Tony nodded as he closed the door, and Sam was alone. Talking to Simon again had been painful. His open hostility and suspicion had wounded her deeply, and she regretted losing her temper with him. She knew full well that if he gave just the slightest hint of forgiving her, or of some kind of reconciliation, she would throw herself at his feet and behave as through nothing had ever come between them.

Not that there was much chance of that. She sighed and ran a hand through her hair. She had hurt Simon more than he had wounded her. Even though her intentions had been more or less honourable, she had still betrayed his trust. Even if she could prove to him that she had been on his side, there was still a rift between them that could probably never be healed.

Though she was reluctant to admit it, she still harboured a hope that if she could save him from whatever was happening to him, then he might forgive her. The hope was hair-thin and as fragile as spun glass, but it was there. She closed her eyes and tried to relax. It had been a busy day and was showing no signs of coming to a conclusion any time soon.

It seemed as though she had closed her eyes for just a second, but her watch told her she had snoozed for the better part of half an hour when she was disturbed by a voice she knew only too well.

Joy buzzed through on the intercom. 'There's a Mr Cornell to see you.'

Sam straightened herself in the chair and tried to look as though she had not just woken up. 'Ask him to come through, please.'

Cornell's anger shone from his face and his manner left Sam in no doubt he was not prepared for social niceties. 'So where is this dangerous insider?' he asked, looking pointedly around the room.

'A colleague took her down to the toilet,' Sam explained. Then a feeling of pure panic rolled over her. 'Oh, shit. That was more than 20 minutes ago.'

'How very convenient,' Cornell drawled. 'Let me guess: has she escaped, do you think? Has your accomplice been overpowered? Or perhaps gone chasing after the mystery insider?'

'Oh, grow up, Simon,' Sam snapped, surprising herself. 'Put that damned hyperactive suspicion of yours on hold for ten minutes. I have had a shitty weekend and a long, tiring day, and I simply cannot be bothered to try to convince you I'm working in your interests any more. You can either come with me and find out what the hell is going on, or fuck off and I'll let the little bitch go.' Sam realised she was almost yelling, and that Cornell was looking shocked. She took a deep breath. 'Your choice.'

Cornell's expression was subtly different. It was only a trace. She might even be imagining it, but she thought she could see a trace of doubt. She quickly quenched the spark of hope that flared in her chest. Not the time, or the place.

'Let's go,' Cornell replied, his voice now missing the bluster and outrage it had held when he entered the room.

The ladies' toilet was just along the hall and down a side passage. As soon as they turned the corner, Sam saw Tony leaning against the wall beside the door. 'I've been waiting for you,' he said, grinning. 'Left my mobile in the office, and the young lady has locked herself in. Didn't want to leave in case she ran for it.'

'What if she got out through the window?'

'And dropped down from the first floor?'

Sam didn't pursue the argument.

Tony hooked a thumb at the door. 'Want me to get her out?'

'Please, but how …?'

Tony took a step away from the door, spun on his left foot and drove his right into the door just above the handle. The door crashed open and there was a startled squeal from within.

'I thought you were going to pick it,' said Sam, but Tony was already inside the washroom and heading for the closed cubicle door. 'No, wait!' Sam yelled as Tony started to turn. Aborting the kick threw him off balance and he stumbled against the wall. Sam offered him an exasperated look as she stood in front of the cubicle door.

'Karen? I know it's you. I also know how cramped it is in there. We need you to come out now, and if you don't, I'll have to let my friend kick this door in too. Now, you might be able to squeeze far enough back so you don't get your kneecaps broken, but I wouldn't bet on it. Would you prefer to come out?'

Sam was just about to call Tony over when they all heard the *snick* of the latch being pulled back, and the door edged slowly open. Karen stepped out of the cubicle and squealed when she saw Cornell standing in front of her.

17

'Perhaps we could return to the office?' Sam suggested.

Tony took a firm grip on Karen's arm, and Sam held out her arm to remind Simon which way to go. As they passed Joy's desk, Sam caught her eye and mimed a request for coffee, then everybody briefly milled around in Hanshaw's office as they found places to sit.

Sam, Karen and Tony took up their previous positions, and Simon found a smaller chair on the opposite side of the room. He and Karen seemed unable to look at each other. Sam worried with her teeth at a fingernail, wondering where she should start. Now that she had most of the important players in one room, it should have been easy to get the ball rolling, but nothing came to her. Cornell unintentionally helped her out.

'There's obviously something going on, but I need more details. For a start, what's she doing here?' He pointed at Karen.

'You know her?' asked Sam.

'Of course I do. Karen Malden. Been with us for about a year.'

'And what's her job?'

'She works in admin and human resources.'

'And what exactly is it your company does, Simon?'

'Software house. We have a product that organisations use to share information confidentially. Totally secure.'

'Now it's Karen's turn,' said Sam.

Karen's face went bright red. 'But I can't tell them …'

'That you serve a mistress? I promise nothing you say will be repeated outside this room.' Sam looked up and fixed Cornell and Tony with steely glares. Both nodded. 'There's, nothing to worry about.'

It took Karen a moment to start, and when she did, she spoke so quietly Sam had trouble hearing her. 'I didn't know what was going on at first. My mistress just told me where to go and gave me an envelope to deliver to Mr Hanshaw. She told me to act like I was rich and powerful, and to pretend that I was acting on behalf of a client. I wasn't told any names and my mistress said not to expect to hear any from Mr Hanshaw. All I knew was that my mistress was having a man investigated, and that I had to visit Mr Hanshaw to pay him and take his report. It wasn't until the third visit that Mr Hanshaw let Mr Cornell's name slip out.'

'That must have been just after the first time I rowed with Hanshaw about you,' Sam told Cornell.

'The *first* time?' A ghost of a smile hovered around Cornell's lips. 'So that would have been the weekend we had Italian?'

Sam nodded and turned her attention back to Karen. 'How did that make you feel?'

'I didn't know what to think. I didn't understand why anybody would have anything against Mr Cornell. Everybody seems to like him at work, and he's always been nice to me.' There was no hint in Karen's face that she was laying it on thick for Cornell's benefit. Sam flicked a look at him and was delighted to see he was embarrassed by the accolade. She prompted Karen for one last piece of information. 'And what did you do after you found out it was Mr Cornell you were helping to have investigated?'

'What could I do? It was my mistress's business, not mine.'

'Tony, you next.'

'Sure,' he said with his usual shrug. 'There's not much to tell. Hanshaw was curious and told me to tail this lady last time she came here. I followed her back to the SCCS offices, then again when she left work. She led me a pretty dance along the A10, then ended up at the place in Botany Bay.'

'I thought that was in Australia,' Cornell interrupted.

'Enfield, near Cruz Hill,' Tony explained. 'I reported back to Hanshaw, and he told me to put eyes on the place. I set myself up at a cable box on the other side of the road and see nothing until some guy in a beat-up Escort rolls into the drive. Fat, ugly bugger with the dress sense of a dog. Looked like a bath wouldn't have hurt him either. The lady there lets him in.' Sam saw Karen hold her breath, and guessed she was wondering if Tony would say anything about what she was wearing. 'An hour later I get moved on by a muscle-brain from the East End ...'

Tony's voice died away and he looked troubled. A moment later he spun around and smashed his open palm onto the wall. Everybody jumped. 'Damn! David fucking Walker. I knew I should have kept looking for him and given the bastard a good kicking.'

'What are you talking about?' Sam asked.

'Hanshaw. Walker must have been told to move me on, but he knows I work for Hanshaw. He must have had someone else add two and two together for him, 'cos he's too fucking stupid to count to four himself. Either he told this girl's boss and she told him to give Hanshaw a warning, or he took it on himself for a laugh. Thing is, he knows where Hanshaw lives.'

'Oh, God.' Sam felt sick. 'Will he have hurt him?'

'Depends on how drunk he was before he got there. He's nasty.'

'Go. Now. Break the bloody door down if you have to.'

Tony didn't answer, just opened the door and hurried out. A shocked silence seemed to ripple out behind him. Cornell caught Sam's eye and raised his eyebrows.

'Hanshaw has been out of contact since Saturday,' Sam explained. 'It not like him.'

Cornell nodded slowly and he looked grim. 'My turn again?'

'If you don't mind.'

'Why should I?' He gave her a very direct look and added, 'Everybody else seems to have been paying a lot more attention to what's been going on around me than I have.'

'Everything helps,' said Sam.

'I set the company up six years ago, with a very good friend. He put in the money and I put in my brains, and we split the stock 50-50. The difference was he was a sleeping partner. Shared the profits but left me to run things.

'He died about three years ago. Company had taken off, but his widow decided to sell her shares. She wanted a lump sum, not a trickle from profits. I tried to buy her out, but a venture capital company offered her way more than I could afford. Way more than the shares were worth. Never got to see anybody from the company, just their solicitors and the person they put in as joint managing director: Diana Cartwright. We've politely detested each other ever since.'

Out of the corner of her eye, Sam saw Karen flinch. 'Different management approach?' she asked Cornell.

'Sort of. She wants to maximise profit, but I won't do that at the expense of quality or security. Spend two years fleecing a customer and they go somewhere else. You end up out of business because you spend all your time trying to drum up new clients. Ideal for a VC, not so good for the rest of us.'

'But you run all aspects of the business jointly?'

Cornell smiled his naughty boy grin and Sam's heart wanted to melt. 'I'm the only one with the codes that allow new releases of the software. That sort of gives me a casting vote.'

Sam went cold. 'Thank you for the information, Simon.' She turned back to Karen. 'I think it's time you told Mr Cornell the name of your mistress.'

Karen's face burned red and she looked at the floor before speaking so softly that Sam almost couldn't hear her: 'Diane Cartwright.'

'That's absurd,' protested Simon, but Sam had eyes only for Karen. 'Besides, Diana Cartwright lives in St Albans. Not this Bombay whatever.'

'Does that rule her out?'

Simon's features creased in concentration. 'Well … perhaps not. For the last year she's had one of my programmers, Ryk Richards, on "secondment," working on a project for the VC. He just happens to be short, overweight, scruffy and of dubious personal habits. Oh, and I think he drives a rat of a Ford.'

Sam drew a deep breath before turning to look at Karen. The girl was huddled in her chair, still looking at the floor. Her hands washed themselves in her lap, and she was making tiny rocking motions. Sam stood and went to her, taking her hands in her own and slowly pulling her to her feet. When the girl wouldn't look up, in a curious echo, Sam put her finger under the girl's chin and lifted her face. There were tears glistening in Karen's eyes, but their gazes locked again and, once more, Sam brushed her thumb across Karen's bottom lip.

'I take no pleasure in this, Karen, but you must see that everything I said is true. If you stay with her she will hurt you, or discard you. You must admit the truth to us so we can try to put things right. Is Diana Cartwright really your mistress?'

Still their eyes held each other's, and Sam almost wept herself when she saw the moment Karen surrendered to her. The girl nodded, just, and Sam kissed her softly on the lips. 'Thank you for your honesty.' She took her hand away from Karen's chin, but kept hold of her hands with the other as she gestured the girl should sit again. 'Now, what else can you tell us about why she wants to harm Mr Cornell?'

Sam flicked a glance at Simon and saw his lips were pursed slightly and he was frowning.

'I don't know anything,' Karen said. 'I just know they are working together.'

'Thank you, Karen,' said Cornell. 'None of this will be held against you, and your job is still there if you want it.'

Karen nodded but couldn't seem to look at him.

'And perhaps I owe you an apology,' he said to

Sam. 'I still don't like that you hid things from me, but perhaps we need to talk. Later, though. I think we should try to clear this up first. May I use your phone?'

Sam pushed it towards him, not trusting herself to speak. He grabbed the handset and started dialling. 'John? Simon. Security lockdown protocol. No, it's not a fucking drill. Right now. Oh, and make sure Richards touches nothing from the moment you get down to his cave … Bugger … When? No, I still want the lockdown, and I want everybody out of the building by the time I get there. Including you. Thanks'

Cornell turned to the others. 'Ryk Richards left the office an hour ago. So did Cartwright. I need to get to the office, find out what they were doing.'

'Or we could go straight to Botany Bay,' Sam suggested, debating if she should mention the cars she saw in the drive as she left The Manse.

'And accuse them of what?'

Sam's mouth opened and closed a couple of times, but she had no argument to offer. 'Let me come with you.'

Cornell thought it over for a few seconds, then reluctantly agreed. 'She has to stay here, though.' He pointed at Karen.

'Why?' Karen asked.

'I don't want to risk you running off to Cartwright as soon as our backs are turned, I don't think it's fair to put you in harm's way, and I think we may be able to use you as a bargaining chip.'

'Sorry, Karen,' said Sam. 'He's talking sense. I'm going to have to borrow those cuffs again.'

'Oh, no.' Karen blushed as Cornell raised his eyebrows.

'Oh, yes, but this time we'll find somewhere more

comfortable for you. I promise if we aren't back soon, I'll get someone to release you.' They compromised on a seat near a radiator, and Sam made sure it was switched off before she slipped one side of the cuffs around a pipe and ratcheted the other around Karen's wrist.

Simon wanted to take his car, but Sam vetoed the idea. He looked at her battered Polo with great scepticism. 'Are you sure it will get us there?'

'It will, and more importantly, nobody there knows it. That thing you drive may as well have a flashing light on the top and a siren screaming "Look at me, look at me."' She offered him a grin, but he didn't respond.

Neither of them spoke on the short drive, and Sam was relieved about that. There was a slight atmosphere, but she had expected that. In fact, she had expected far worse, and wasn't sure if it was because Simon was in the process of forgiving her, or because he was simply preoccupied by what might be going on at his offices. She decided not to ask; in this case ignorance might well be bliss.

'That's the wrong way,' said Simon as he saw she was about to turn down a side road. 'Next right, not this one.'

'I'm playing a hunch,' said Sam, reaching for her phone. 'And I want to see if I can get Tony here too.'

'He could be a while.' Cornell protested. 'I think I'll just trot over and –'

Sam held up her hand and spoke into her phone for a few minutes. 'Three is better than two,' she said when she had hung up. 'And I like longer odds if I can get them. Tony said he can be here in 20 minutes, 15 if he gets lucky.'

'Is your boss okay?'

The question surprised Sam. She hadn't expected Cornell to care. 'He'll live. He'd been left bound up with duct tape. Messed his bed, dehydrated and hungry. Pissed off more than hurt.'

Cornell nodded, then went on: 'How about a compromise? We'll wait the 15 minutes, then go in even if he hasn't arrived. I have to find out what those two have been up to in there.'

Sam thought the offer over. She wasn't keen on the idea, but if it kept Simon from rushing off right now, it was better than nothing. 'Deal.'

She killed the engine and the lights, then switched the radio on, turning down the volume and picking a commercial classical music station that struggled to make snatches of symphonies sound like properly-produced tracks as it sliced them up with scattered adverts for double glazing and the like.

The music was Sam's way of trying to make the missing conversation less obvious. Simon stared out through the windscreen and she tapped her fingers on the steering wheel, out of time with the music she wasn't really listening to. Her ears filtered out the DJ's inane babble until the words 'selection of jazz classics' broke through. A moment later a sliding clarinet note that she knew led into Gershwin's 'Rhapsody in Blue' had her finger stabbing at the buttons on the front of the radio. The music changed to '90s pop. Sam felt a lump in her throat so big it almost stopped her breathing, and tears pricked at her eyes. She tried to look at Cornell from the corner of her eye, but it was difficult to see anything in the dingy light of the cloudy afternoon. She could have been seeing what she hoped to, but she thought he looked sad.

'Simon, I –'

She wanted to talk. She wanted to apologise to him over and over and try to claw back at least some of what they once had. Her words stuck in her throat as Cornell slowly shook his head.

'Not now, Sam.'

At least he had not said no. Not exactly. She began to feel uncomfortable again. Their proximity felt wrong after the musical reminder. Tony seemed to be taking forever.

18

Sam spotted Tony's motorbike heading toward the car park just as Cornell's grace period expired. 'There he is!' said Cornell, but Sam couldn't tell how much of his eagerness was wanting to get into the building and how much was just wanting to get out of the car. She started the engine and drove quietly, without lights, into the car park. Tony had stopped out of sight of the front door and Sam pulled up next to him. He was still removing his crash helmet and looked like he was itching for an excuse to hit somebody. 'I left Hanshaw running a bath and trying to eat his whole fridge,' he explained. 'Let's do what we have to do here. I have business elsewhere.'

Simon started tapping at a keypad next to the main doors. Several minutes later, he slammed the glass panel nearest the keypad and turned back to face them. 'Fucking thing won't unlock.'

Tony examined the door for a moment. 'What if it wasn't locked in the first place?'

'Of course it's locked. That's the last thing in the procedure for a lockdown.'

'Funny how it's open then,' said Tony, pulling the

door wide. No alarms sounded. 'Who else has the code?'

Cornell counted on his fingers. 'Me, my PA, John, the receptionist, Cart … Oh.'

Tony looked grim. 'We may have a reception committee.'

'How many?' Sam asked.

'No way of knowing. Depends how many of us they are expecting.'

'One,' said Sam, after a moment's thought. 'She'll expect us to be doing a covert snoop, figuring we'll have found out where Karen worked. She won't expect us to know who she is.' She looked at Simon. 'And she'll expect it to be you, given that you ordered the lockdown.'

'If they just want to kill whoever comes, or give him a kicking, it'll be two blokes,' Tony guessed. 'If they want to grab him and take him away, three. They wouldn't leave their own car in the car park, 'cos that would show they were there.'

'Makes sense,' Sam nodded and turned to Cornell. 'Can you look after yourself? Might get nasty. They won't fight by any rules.'

'I might even enjoy it,' Cornell said with feeling. Tony grinned at him and quietly slapped him on the shoulder. 'My office is the second left from the door at the top of the stairs,' Cornell added. 'I go in first.'

Sam drew breath to argue, but Cornell insisted. 'They are going to be expecting me. If I can distract them, you two get better options.'

Simon swiped them through the door at the bottom of the stairs. Through the glass of another set of doors ahead of them Sam saw that the building was in a twilight gloom, with occasional monitors casting pools of blue light. She pursed her lips. That could work against them if it was the same above.

Simon pointed to the stairs and strode purposefully up them. Sam and Tony followed, stepping softly to preserve the fiction that only Simon was in the building. He waited for them at the door and mimed that they mustn't let it shut after he went through. Sam nodded. Cornell swiped his card, pushed the door open and strode in.

Sam caught the door with the toe of her shoe and winced. Not because the door pinched her foot, but because she was still dressed in her outfit from that morning, complete with the heels. It seemed impossible, but she had actually forgotten she was wearing them. As she wondered what to do about them, there was a crash from inside and a hubbub of raised voices. Tony slammed into the door beside her, throwing it open and rushing into the melee.

There was fighting somewhere in the room, but Sam couldn't see who was involved or where it was happening. She fumbled at the wall by the door and a lightning storm filled the room as half the fluorescent strips flickered into life. Simon was on the floor, struggling with somebody who was trying to force a baseball bat across his throat. Tony, screaming his anger and needing to hurt somebody, was already half way there.

A second man was lying against a desk with his head at an uncomfortable angle. Sam didn't think his neck was broken, but he didn't seem too keen on playing any further part in the action. Sam looked around, trying to figure out what she could do to help and checking for anybody not yet involved in the fight.

Tony had launched himself at the man trying to throttle Simon, knocking him aside and trying to rip the bat from his hands. Simon seemed to be out of things for a moment, curled up on the floor holding his neck. Tony and the other man had rolled off in opposite directions and both were now on their feet again. Tony had lost the tussle for the baseball bat and was now busy avoiding sweeping strokes from it.

A shadow moved in one of the offices, flickering in the corner of Sam's vision. She crept around the wall, staying out of sight as much as she could, then waited just to the side of the doorway. Almost the instant she got there, a third man yelled and ran out of the office, swinging another baseball bat and looking to take Tony from behind. Sam stuck out her foot and tripped him. The bat flew from the man's hand and went almost straight up as he stumbled forward and hit his head against a partition. He was still moving but seemed in no hurry to get up.

The thug confronting Tony was swinging his bat viciously, leaving Sam in no doubt he intended to kill with it, or at least do serious damage. Tony had made a mistake and let himself get cornered in a narrow space between two rows of desks. Tony was holding him off, just, with a backrest that had broken off a chair. Sam slipped out of her heels and then, still holding them in one hand, eased closer, staying out of the thug's sight-line, until she was able to plant a spinning hook kick to his arm. She could have punched it into his neck – just – but she wanted to incapacitate him, not kill him. He screamed as he dropped the bat, staggering sideways and turning to face her. His right arm hung limply, but his left was outstretched, the hand clawing for her throat, as his face contorted in rage. Sam waited for him to come inside her reach, then stepped sideways and jabbed him in the solar plexus with stiff fingers. He folded like a cardboard cut-out and lay gasping for breath on the floor.

While Sam had been busy helping Tony, the man she had tripped up had recovered enough to rejoin the fight. However, Simon had already picked up the fallen baseball bat and was swinging it at him, backing him towards the door until he stumbled, turned and ran. Sam could see Simon consider giving chase, but then decide to let him go. Bat still in hand, he started searching desks until he found a roll of parcel tape, which he used to strap up the men on the floor.

'Nice job,' said Tony, breathing hard. 'I'd have left the shoes on though. With those heels you could have stabbed the bastard in the heart. If he had one.'

'Why?'

Tony pointed to the thug that had been trying to kill him. 'Because that's Dave Walker. He's the bastard that left Hanshaw to die.' He turned away and took out his phone.

Cornell pointed at a nearby door. 'Right, shall we start ripping her office apart?'

Sam grinned at Tony, who had now finished his call. 'We should get jobs like this more often.'

He smiled back. 'I'm going to leave you to this for a bit. I've got some mates coming round. We're going to have a little chat with Walker.'

'Don't kill him,' Sam said, taking Tony's arm and making sure that he looked at her. 'We don't want any more complications in this case. And don't leave. I might need you.'

'Promise,' said Tony, but his eyes were hard and unforgiving. 'But Hanshaw's been a good boss for years. Walker needs that explaining to him.'

Sam and Cornell set to work, turning out every

drawer and every file in Diana Cartwright's office. Every cabinet was opened, by force where necessary. Within five minutes Sam knew they were wasting their time. 'This place is as clean as the house,' she complained. 'The bitch knows what she's doing. Nothing but routine stuff.'

'Then let's go pay a visit to Mr Richards' little empire,' Cornell suggested, rising from the desk. 'Tony, grab a swipe card from the top drawer of my desk. It will let you move around the building when your friends come.' Tony nodded and walked away. Cornell led Sam down the stairs.

Richards' office was one of four along the far wall of an otherwise open-plan environment. Only his had the blinds down and closed. The fetid air of the room made Sam feel sick as soon as they opened the door. 'I think I'll wait outside,' she said. 'There's nothing but the computer in there anyway.'

While Sam stood in the doorway, Cornell rooted around inside the room. There was only one desk, and the drawers proved to be empty apart from some half-eaten pizza and a mug with fur growing in the bottom. On top of the desk were four reference books, an oversize monitor and a computer to match. Simon pulled all the wires from the back of the machine and picked it up. 'You're right, and there's no need for us to stay in this festering pit.' He led her back up to his own office.

Sam sat at Cornell's desk while he worked at the PC on a side table. She saw the screen flicker into life, and then Simon started muttering. She got the occasional word, a partial phrase, but her mind started to wander. She still dangled the heels from her hand, and had propped her feet up on Simon's desk. She looked at her feet. The stockings were 'fully fashioned' with darker heel and toe, and a band running between them along her sole. The desk was a nice height. She could sit on it, Simon in his chair, her toes running along the bulge in his trousers until he had to open them so she could wrap her feet softly around …

The word 'bastard', spoken with vitriol, jarred her back into the real world. 'Problem?' she asked.

'There's nothing here.' Cornell was staring at her feet, which were tightly arched. She tried not to blush, and hoped nothing of her daydream had been visible. She hid a smile as she saw him force his mind back to the point. 'He must have kept everything on an external storage device, like a mini hard drive or a memory stick.'

'Oh. Crap.'

'Don't panic yet. There's something else I can try.' He came back to his desk and waited until she got the hint and gave him back his chair. 'We take snapshots of all the development boxes every hour or so, like mini-backups, and that includes attached devices. The idiots kept losing so much data … Anyway, we never broadcast the fact that we were doing this, so he might not have known that it was there.' He clattered at the keyboard for a few moments, muttering under his breath again, then hissed: 'Gotcha!'

'You found something.'

'I found all of it. It's a week or so old, but it's enough that I can see what he was doing. Looks like he had some kind of phage virus working its way back through the copies. I got there before it could delete everything.'

'So we know what they were up to?'

'We will when I've had a chance to read it.'

Sam looked over his shoulders as he started flicking through folders, opening files here and there, all in silence. Then he opened a folder and cursed. 'What a dick. He has a document called "Diary of the Overlord". Please tell me I didn't employ someone that stupid?' He clicked on the icon and a password request came up. 'At least he encrypted it.'

'So we can't get in?'

'Mere mortals, no, but I am no mere mortal.' Simon worked more technomagic and the screen started to flicker. Sam's eyes began to hurt and she looked away. 'Cracker app,' said Cornell, as though that explained everything. 'Could take a couple of minutes, could take an hour or so.'

Sam perched on Cornell's desk, more or less facing him, and put her shoes next to her. Crossing her left ankle over her right knee, she started to massage her foot, paying particular attention to the fleshy pad behind her toes. 'Starting to ache,' she explained, slipping the shoe back on. 'Exquisite torture if I couldn't take them off.'

Simon returned a thin smile, but his eyes didn't seem to join in. Sam put on the other shoe and retreated to a chair on the other side of the room.

About half an hour later there was a triumphant fanfare from the computer. Cornell all but ran to the machine and started scrolling through the file. Sam tried to keep up but the text was moving too fast for her. She could see a lot of bad words, and several references to Karen and what Richards was planning to do to her. The man's mind made her feel almost as sick as the smell in his office. There was technical jargon, too, but none that made any sense. Cornell was silent, but she could feel tension building around him.

'From scanning this it looks like they think they have something that can influence people through images flashed on their computer screen.'

'Subminimal images?'

'Subliminal. Sort of. The basic idea is from the '50s, but it never really worked. Seems like they think they've made it more effective. Even so, I wouldn't have said it would be reliable.'

'So what was he going to do with it?'

'I'm not sure, but I think they were looking for a way to inject it into my product.' His looked furious. 'I don't appreciate people messing with my things.'

'Well, how much harm could they do?'

'You don't understand, Sam. This product is all over the place: banks, police, courts, inland revenue, health service. If they could find a way to influence people using it …'

'So how do we stop them?'

'That's the mad part. They're already stopped. Only I have the code that enables new software or feature releases. Otherwise it's as tight as a nun's …' He stopped, coughed, and tried again. 'They have no way to deliver it.'

'What happens if you die,' Sam asked, slowly.

'Failsafe. There is a back-up copy of the release key with my solicitors. I die, they release it to the most senior executive of the company.' His voice tailed off again.

'That's why she was trying to take over the company,' said Sam. 'She would get the codes, and this thing would be let out into the world. Could she hack into the solicitors?'

'Wouldn't do any good. I gave it to them in an envelope. Someone would have to break in physically, then burgle their safe.'

'Someone like Mr Walker?'

Simon looked worried for a moment, 'Perhaps.'

'Is there any other way to get the code? Something like that … cracker app you used?'

Cornell shook his head. 'It would need a brute force attack into the datacentre. At least a dozen servers running for weeks. Maybe years.'

'How many servers could you get in two of those computer cabinets, the ones a bit taller than you? Because I saw two of them at the house, in Botany Bay.'

Cornell raked his hand through his hair. 'Not good. We could shut the system down at the datacentre, but who knows what that would do to the users? I don't really want the hospitals losing half their patient records.'

'Why not shut them down at the source? Go to the house. They probably aren't even there, and I still have Karen's keys.'

'I'll drive, you navigate.'

19

'Why don't we just drive right in?' Cornell protested as Sam parked her Polo in the same side road she had used before.

Sam had talked Simon out of driving, fearing he might fry the engine. She could feel his impatience to get on with whatever had to be done. 'Driving up to the front door would be a bit conspicuous,' she pointed out.

'She'll be expecting us anyway,' he replied.

'We don't know that,' chipped in Tony from the back seat. 'Walker won't have got back to her, so she'll be in the dark.'

'We don't know what we are going to face in there,' added Sam. 'No point throwing away the tiny advantage we might get from sneaking in. Now, shall we go or do you want to chat some more?' She added a sweet smile to barb the point.

'You were much nicer when you knew your place,' Cornell grumbled.

'I still do,' she said softly, looking directly into his eyes and holding his gaze. Simon cocked his head to one side, brow furrowing slightly, but said nothing. He pulled the door handle and left the car before Sam could say anything else. Not that she had anything else to say. She would have loved the right words to spring to her lips, but all that happened was a tiny little bud of hope stuck in her throat. She climbed out of the car and waved for Tony to follow.

From the road, the front of the house looked dark and uninhabited, but Cartwright's Audi and Richards' rolling rust bucket were both in the drive. Sam got Simon and Tony to duck down into the cover of the shrubs along the wall as soon as she could, then led them around until they could come at the house from the side.

They still had to scoot along the front wall of the house – Sam only had keys for the front door – and it was only when they were that close to the windows that they could see a faint, telltale glow behind some of them; indirect lighting from a hall, or from a room at the back of the house. Someone was definitely home. Although an empty house would have been easier to tackle, Sam felt a small satisfaction that Cartwright and Richards seemed still to be there. It presented an opportunity for payback.

She worked the Chubb in the mortise first, but found it was already unlocked. She then offered the other key up to the cylinder. A twist and a soft click later, the door eased open a crack. Sam looked back over her shoulder. 'Is everybody ready?'

Two heads nodded slowly and she started to push the door open wide enough for them to slip through. Almost instantly, Sam felt uneasy. A prickle ran up her backbone and goose-bumps flared on her forearms. A single light shone from the far end of the hall, but every door off the hall had been left open onto darkened rooms. An army could have been hiding there.

'How do we want to play this?' Tony whispered.

'Room by room or straight to the problem?'

'Let's try and get to the servers,' Cornell replied. 'If there's trouble here, it can come find us. We could waste an hour chasing shadows.'

Sam strained her eyes to try to see into every darkened room at the same time as she led the two men along the hall. They were almost up to the door that led to the dungeon when she heard something she had been expecting ever since they moved away from the front door; three sharp clicks from a woman's heels as she stepped into the hall behind them. The three metallic clicks that followed, those of the hammer being pulled back on a sidearm, she had not expected. Sam froze.

'That will be far enough,' said the crisp, precisely enunciated voice of Diane Cartwright. 'All of you face me, then take two steps away from the door.'

Sam did as she was told, then realised she had reacted automatically to the tone of command Cartwright had used. Her face burned as she turned to face the woman. In the dim light she saw that Cartwright was wearing a sharp business suit and her trademark killer heels. Her posture, her face, everything about her radiated command and control, just as much as the small semi-automatic in her right hand. Sam focused on the gun, and tried to block out the crazy voice at the back of her mind that said she should be doing anything this woman said.

Sam didn't like guns, and had as little to do with them as possible. In her line of work, though, she had made it her business to find out the basics. It was a .22; not a man-stopper, but a bullet to the head would kill someone just as dead, and a body-shot could cause someone bleed to death before they could get help. Cartwright, though, appeared not to know much about guns and was holding the weapon almost casually.

'Diane, what the hell are you doing?' Cornell pushed past Sam. 'What is this all about?'

'Money, of course. And power.'

'You want a raise?'

'Very droll. I'm sure you realise the stakes here are far in excess of the petty amounts of cash your business is capable of generating.'

'Very melodramatic,' Cornell replied. 'I suppose you are now going to reveal your ingenious master plan to us, then shoot us.'

Sam willed Simon to keep the woman talking. Something seemed out of place. She hadn't worked out what it was – yet – but she had a hunch that it was fairly important.

'Cornell, either your playboy lifestyle has gone to your head, or you have been watching too many action movies. However, since you asked so nicely, I shall tell you what I have been working on. You've heard of subliminal suggestion, of course?'

Sam mentally crossed her fingers. Simon could blow everything if he let on how much they already knew. She almost let out a sigh of relief when he played Cartwright along, pretending they knew next to nothing. He let her blather on for minutes, and all the time Sam tried to figure out what it was she had subconsciously noticed. Heard! She realised it was something she had heard. Or not heard?

She started to run, straight at Cartwright. Simon yelled at her. Cartwright yelled at her to get back. Sam focused on the gun, on Cartwright's finger inside the trigger guard. She saw the finger start to tighten on the trigger and jinked right, into Cartwright's weak side. On the next step she went forward into a roll. She heard a click, then Cartwright's scream of frustration. The hammer was cocked again, but then she was crashing into Cartwright's legs and the woman was tumbling on top of her and Sam was trying to stop her roll and turn around before Cartwright could …

Heavier steps, a scuff, a scream of pain, and the sound of metal skidding across marble floor. Sam was up on her knees, trying to see in every direction at once. Cornell was standing over Cartwright. Actually, he was standing *on* Cartwright, pinning her wrist to the floor with his foot. Sam turned her head and looked for the weapon. It was about five feet away from her, against the wall. She rose, crossed to it, picked it up. When she looked back at Simon she could see he was breathing hard. 'Christ, you like to take chances,' he gasped.

Sam grinned. 'Calculated risk. From the way she was holding the gun, I realised she wasn't used to it. Anybody who knows anything will clear a gun when they aren't using it; take out the clip and jack the round out of the chamber. I realised I'd only heard her cock the hammer.' Sam pulled the slide and let it snap back into place. 'Can't fire a gun if it isn't loaded. I took a chance that there was no round in the chamber, and that she wouldn't be able to hit the side of a moving bus anyway. I got lucky twice.'

Tony said nothing, his face white. Cornell shook his head. 'You have issues.' He took his foot off Cartwright's wrist and hauled her to her feet. 'What do we do about her?'

Cartwright looked wary but not panicked, and Sam guessed she knew perfectly well that it would be difficult for Simon to explain a corpse. Sam flicked the Walther's safety catch on, then stuffed it into the waistband of her skirt before grabbing the front of

Cartwright's blouse.

This woman had fucked her up. She had, ultimately, fucked her and Simon up. If it hadn't been for her, Sam would never have met Simon and she wouldn't be in this mess anyway. And then there was Karen. Sam's anger reached white-hot as she thought of what the woman had done to that poor, trusting little idiot. The voice that had told Sam she should obey this woman crawled away into the back of her mind and disappeared. 'I don't like you,' she spat through gritted teeth.

'Let me go,' blustered Cartwright, stuttering, confidence failing now she was looking into Sam's eyes.

'You use people, bitch. You treat them like pieces on a game board, and don't give a damn about them. I have a present for you. Several. One from someone who respected you too much to even think about doing something like this, and another from someone you left to die.'

Sam smashed her fist into Cartwright's face, a right hook crashing into her jaw, and heard a distinct crack. Keeping the momentum for the backswing, she hit her again, this time back-handed across the right cheek. Then she let go of her blouse. It had been a last-second decision not to just ram the heel of her open palm into the woman's face. A broken nose would have been guaranteed, but it might also have brought her back to the dead body situation again. Cartwright dropped like a rock.

'Are we going to just stand here or are we going to stop this virus thing?' she snapped, then started walking towards the door to the dungeon. Released from their paralysis, the two men spun to follow her.

At the bottom of the stairs, Tony seemed taken

aback, or fascinated, by the dungeon equipment, and even Cornell seemed to be looking around with professional interest. Sam thumped Tony on the arm. 'No time for that now. Over there.'

She pointed to the door and Tony pushed it. 'Locked,' he reported.

'Unlock it then,' Sam replied, and sounded exasperated. Tony grinned and aimed a kick at the lock. The door smashed open.

Ryk Richards cowered at the desk, but there was a satisfied smirk on his face. 'You can do what you like to me, but you're too late. The system is working on the last shell and you can't stop it.'

'Lose him,' Cornell snapped to Tony, who dragged Richards bodily out. The programmer's whining protests could be heard from the next room, but neither Cornell nor Sam paid them any attention. There came a slapping sound, then another, and the protests stopped.

Cornell had already dropped into Richards' chair and was hammering at the keyboard. 'Can't get in,' he muttered. 'Little fuck has locked the keyboard.'

'Can't Tony encourage him to unlock it?'

'No time.' Cornell pointed to the screen where four green bars were topped by a fifth that was rapidly changing from red to green. 'The keyboard will be locked, then the session above that will be locked, and so on. If he had a clue we might be coming to stop him, the little bastard will have tangled this up so badly that even he couldn't stop it in time.'

'So what happens?'

'This thing breaks the access codes in about 15 minutes, then the virus they've created gets uploaded to my core servers in Docklands, and from there to the customers.' He sighed. 'I guess I'd better make some phone calls and try to stop people using the systems.' He reached in his pocket and pulled out a mobile. 'Damn, no signal.'

'Can't we just switch them off?' Sam asked.

'Cabinets are locked.'

Sam looked around the room. There was a grey box on the wall just behind the two screens that had been used to monitor the things being done to Karen, and on the box was a large chrome-handled switch, padlocked in place. There were warning symbols and lightning flashes all over it. Wishing for at least a .38, Sam pulled the little pistol out of her waistband, slipped off the safety and started firing.

The first round cracked the box. The second broke the padlock. The third seemed to have no effect, but the fourth and fifth cause showers of sparks. Sam kept pulling the trigger until the slide jammed open, oblivious to the fact that the computers had stopped some time before. Simon put his hand over the little gun and eased it from her grasp. 'Unconventional, but effective.'

'It worked?'

He nodded.

20

They collected Tony and Richards on the way out, but by the time they got back to the hallway, Cartwright had disappeared.

'Damn,' Sam grumbled. 'I must be getting soft. No way should she have got up from that.'

'Shame,' Cornell agreed. 'I had a few questions for her. Tony, would you mind taking *this*' – he pointed at Ryk Richards – 'somewhere for a moment. I need to have a chat with him later.'

Tony nodded and gave Ryk's arm a shake. As he led the subdued programmer off in the direction of the kitchen, he looked back over his shoulder. 'Not too long though, eh? I have something similar to do with Walker.'

'You probably wouldn't have got many answers from Cartwright,' said Sam. 'She didn't strike me as the co-operative type.'

'So what now? The police?'

'That's up to you.' Sam was very conscious of the fact they were alone again. So much needed to be said, but she wasn't sure how to start.

'How so?' Simon's forehead furrowed slightly.

'You're the injured party, aren't you? Hanshaw will be happy enough to come down on your side, as will I. You could have a case against her.'

'But what about this virus business, and what about him?' Cornell hooked a thumb at Richards.

Sam shrugged. 'The police might listen to you, if you can actually make them understand what you're talking about. Or you could just get them to send his PC for forensic analysis. I'll bet there's all sorts of stuff on there to get him in trouble. Besides, isn't he the only guy who knows how to crack your security?'

Simon nodded, scowling. 'And knowing my luck I couldn't even fire him without an employment tribunal doing me for unfair dismissal.'

Sam smiled at him. 'I had better get back to the office and see if I can get myself out of a false imprisonment claim.'

'What?'

'Karen. She could easily sue the ass off me. Don't think she will, though.'

'Why not?'

'Just a hunch. Want a lift back to the agency?'

Cornell took a few private moments with Richards then kicked him out of the house, after making sure he had no keys to regain access. Sam locked up and drove Cornell to Hanshaw's office. By the time they got there it was almost nine o'clock.

'I expect they'll be gone by now,' said Sam. 'I did tell Joy to let her go at nine.'

'Maybe not,' said Cornell. 'There are still lights on.'

'Probably just Joy waiting to make sure I haven't forgotten my keys.'

Neither seemed to have anything else to say, yet neither made any move to get out of the car. Sam knew they had more ground to cover, and she had a feeling that unless they covered that ground now, they never would. When Simon started fidgeting, she knew she would have to speak up or get out.

'We still need to talk,' she said.

'Perhaps'

'We won't know until we try.'

Cornell wouldn't meet her eyes. 'I don't know. I still have a lot to get straight in my head.'

'Even now? I know what I did was wrong, but I was hoping you could see it was for the right reasons. I can't keep apologising forever.'

'I know, and I know I treated you more harshly than I should have. But there is still a matter of trust. I don't see how we can just pick things up where we left off.'

'Why not?'

'Is that what you're offering?'

Sam surprised herself by hesitating. The word 'yes' had been poised behind her teeth, waiting for the opportunity to be said. Was she having second thoughts? 'That's why I think we need to talk,' she replied finally.

Simon sighed, and Sam knew she had said the wrong thing. He pulled the handle to release the door.

'You know my number, Simon. Ring me, either way.' She got out of the car and closed the door.

Cornell gave her a tentative wave, and she smiled back before he walked to his own motor and drove slowly away. Sam watched the car until it turned the corner to head back to Enfield, hoping every second that she would see the flash of brake lights.

Something inside her died when the car vanished.

Cornell would never make that call. She wished him luck, and hoped his 'club fishing' hobby would help heal the damage they had caused each other. Firmly closing that chapter of her life, she pulled open the door to Hanshaw's office.

She was not surprised to see Joy there. She was surprised to see her sharing a cup of tea with Karen, who was unfettered.

'About time,' said Joy. 'We were beginning to think something unpleasant might have happened.'

'It did, sort of. Did Tony fill you in on Hanshaw?'

Joy pulled a face and nodded. 'Nasty business. Still, came out all right in the end. Are you leaving now?'

'I suppose so.'

Joy looked pointedly at Sam, then at Karen, before leaving her desk to fetch her coat and bag. Sam didn't need the reminder. She had been trying to think of what to do with Karen since she had walked into the office.

'Karen, I think you should come with me.'

'Where?'

'Let's start with something to eat, maybe. I don't know about you, but I'm starving.'

Sam drove them to a fast food joint that did a half-decent fried chicken and they took a table in a quiet corner.

'Do you mind if I ask what happened?' said Karen, pecking nervously at her food.

'Not at all,' said Sam. 'You have a right to know.'

She quickly sketched in the main events of the night and the parts people had played. It took most of the meal, and they were nearing the end of their coffees before she finished. Karen had been raptly attentive throughout, as though she had been watching a thriller movie. The conclusion, though, seemed to shock her more than it ought.

'So she just left?'

'I assume so. When we came out of the computer room, she was gone, and the Audi had gone from the drive. We didn't search the house, though. Judging by what I saw there this afternoon, she had nothing there to leave behind.'

'Except me,' said Karen. Her voice was very small and tears glistened in her eyes.

Sam was stunned. 'You can't seriously be pining after that woman.'

'I suppose not,' Karen shrugged. 'It just feels a little strange being on my own.'

'At least you have the house to yourself.'

Karen shook her head and her eyes opened wide. 'I can't go back there. Not tonight. Not alone. What if she came back? What if she blamed me?' Her voice got louder and Sam saw people flick glances at them. At the same time she suddenly realised neither of them was really dressed properly for the venue. She put her hand on Karen's arm to quiet her.

'I wouldn't put it past her. Are you going to go back to Reading?'

'There's nothing for me there. Even if I could go back, I could hardly turn up like this. I was going to ask if you knew of a cheap hotel. I have a little money, and I think I still have my job.'

'I'll roast Cornell alive if you haven't,' muttered Sam, 'and I'm damned if you're staying in some flea-pit hotel. Come back to my place. We can sort something there for a couple of nights.'

'That's really kind of you, but I'll be fine,' Karen demurred.

'Don't argue,' said Sam, forcefully. 'It's the least I can do.'

Karen gave her a strange, weak smile, but her eyes looked haunted.

During the drive home, Karen seemed to have turned in on herself, and Sam ground her teeth gently in frustration. The art of talking in cars seemed to be dying out, so she passed the drive listening to the radio – carefully tuned to bland '90s pop.

Karen was still acting like her favourite dog had died when they reached Sam's flat, and Sam began to wonder if she had done the right thing. It had been a long, hectic day and all she wanted to do was take a deep bath and climb into bed. Now she could do neither while Karen looked so miserable.

'Is something troubling you?' she asked eventually, and with what she thought was commendable restraint. Karen began to sniffle and Sam groaned inwardly. Not tears, please. It didn't come to that, quite, but Karen's voice was husky and there were hints she was choking back occasional sobs. 'I'm sorry. I don't mean to be a nuisance. I'm frightened.'

'Of what?''

'Everything.'

'Are you going to expand on that?' Sam felt sorry for the girl, even though she was trying not to.

'I'm afraid of being on my own.'

'We all are, Karen.'

'You don't understand. I met my mis ... I mean Miss Cartwright, just after I left college. I've been with her ever since. I've never had to look after myself.

'It won't be so bad. You have your job, and it

shouldn't be too difficult to find a nice little flat somewhere. Once you start getting out and enjoying yourself, you'll wonder what all the fuss was about.' Sam had risen from the couch and crossed to the armchair. She perched on the arm next to Karen and gently stroked her hair.

'I'm afraid of people. I don't know how to react to them. I was always told what to do to people, or what to let them do to me.'

'It's called being shy.'

'I feel useless without my mis ...' Karen bit the word off and let her head fall onto Sam's thigh. Sam felt for her. What this girl was going through had to be ten times worse than the loss she herself was feeling over Simon.

She put her hand on Karen's shoulder. 'I really do understand.'

'How? How can you possibly know?'

Sam took a deep breath. 'Because the same thing happened to me a few days ago, only it was my fault. I gave myself to somebody, like you, then I did something stupid and deceitful and he threw me out. I suppose I deserved it, but nothing ever hurt me as much as that did. Is still doing. I know your hurt is much deeper. I just wanted you to know that someone understood.'

'Who was the man?'

'You don't need to know that.'

'It was Mr Cornell, wasn't it? I thought there was something between you two earlier.'

Sam went bright red, but felt compelled to tell the truth. She had started it, she should finish it. 'Yes, it was him.'

'Funny, but I thought you were a mistress too. Earlier, in the office, when you ...'

'Are you disappointed I'm not?'

'Not yet?'

'Pardon?'

'You never know until you try, and I think you're a natural.' Karen sounded happy and more at ease with herself, and was smiling. She pulled herself up from the chair and turned to face Sam.

'Are you trying to make a point,' Sam asked, feeling shy herself.

'Do I really have to spell it out?'

Sam thought about it for a moment, then decided Karen was being obvious enough. 'I guess I never really thought about it.'

Karen's smile became mischievous, bordering on wicked, as she undid her jacket and placed it on the sofa. In the dim light of Sam's lounge the blouse was less transparent, but Sam was sure she saw the hint of an unnatural line beneath it. The skirt came off next, revealing six suspenders holding up stockings and a stainless steel chastity belt. Then, Karen slowly undid the blouse, holding it closed until all the buttons were undone. 'Doesn't this tempt you?' She slowly opened the blouse to show she was still wearing the nipple clamps Sam had put on her hours before, the silver chain between them contrasting starkly against the black of the corset.

'When did you put those back on?' Sam asked.

'You never told me I could take them off,' Karen replied. She placed the blouse on the sofa, then sank to her knees in front of Sam. She placed her hands on her head, and spread her knees two feet apart. 'I've been locked in this thing all day, and all I have been able to think about all day is you, mistress.'

'But, I …' Sam began to protest her innocence, but

then realised she had made a rod for her own back. She had to admit that the girl looked delicious in such a submissive position, and she remembered how hot she had made herself tormenting the girl earlier. The problem was, she was also imagining herself kneeling there. 'Undress me,' she said, almost without thinking.

'By your mercy, mistress,' said Karen, rising to her feet and obviously trying not to look too pleased with herself. Sam caught her by the arm, her grip perhaps a little too hard, and Karen suddenly looked a little afraid.

'Never say that again,' said Sam. 'A simple yes will do.'

Karen nodded and quickly undressed Sam, who took a secret delight in the girl's expression as each new secret was revealed, especially the lack of knickers. 'Do you always dress like that for work?'

Sam chuckled. 'Sorry, no. Though I might start.'

'You should, you look beautiful.'

'It's pretty much all the lingerie I have.'

Karen looked disappointed. 'I had so many nice things back at the house. Tomorrow, could we …?'

Sam placed her finger on Karen's lips, then gently pushed her down to her knees. Sam sat on the armchair, legs apart, and her mobile chirped. It was within reach and, out of extraordinarily bad habit, she picked it up. A text from an unknown number. She swiped the screen. All that came up was the word 'Italian?' Sam dropped the phone on the table and crooked a finger at Karen. 'Let's focus on tonight.'

As Karen's face disappeared between her thighs, Sam wondered if she could find a paperclip to pick the lock on the chastity belt.

About the Author

Roberta Steele lives in London with her partner. Always a lover of racy romance, she tried her hand at writing and was published on several fan sites. She wrote 'Byte Me' and eventually got up the nerve to send it to somebody when she saw that Telos Moonrise were looking for submissions.

Roberta is a Pisces, loves the water and has a thing about shoes. She loves spaghetti, Sancerre, and Spike – not necessarily in that order.

OTHER TELOS MOONRISE TITLES

Coming soon ...

<u>**Romantic Encounters**</u>

<u>Helen McCabe</u>
The Price of Love
Love in Hiding
In Search of Love
Hostage to Love
When Love Rides Out
Highway of Fear
A Garden Fair
The House on the Mountain

<u>Juliette Benzoni</u>
Catherine: One Love is Enough
Catherine
Belle Catherine
Catherine and Arnaud
Catherine and a Time for Love
A Snare for Catherine
La Dame de Montsalvy